C000080049

Chapter 1
The flood
Florence 4th November 1966

Dante once called the Arno 'that damned accursed ditch'. How prescient he was.

It came as a roaring, roiling mass of dark, muddy fluvial water, cascading through the narrow streets, plunging deep into cellars, sweeping all before it. Travelling at 60 kilometres per hour, the cataclysmic deluge ripped out gas, electricity and water supplies, including the hospital emergency generators, and then ruptured oil tanks, mixing the oil therein with the toxic melange of water, animal carcasses and mud. Cars were swept away like toys and the citizens of Florence fled to the heights of their homes to avoid drowning. Not all succeeded; thirty five people lost their lives. At its height, in Piazza Santa Croce, the waters reached over 6.7 metres high. In the basilica, a crucifix by Cimabue and a 'Last Supper' by Vasari were submerged.

Beautiful furniture from museums and palazzos floated down the Arno past the Ponte Vecchio. At the baptistery, Ghiberti's magnificent East doors, the 'Gates of Paradise', were buckled and stuck in the mud, half their gilded bronze panels ripped out by the torrent. Twenty seven thousand square feet of frescoes in the city's churches and civic buildings were damaged.

Florence was on its knees.

The autumn storms had been even heavier than usual that year. A third of Tuscany's annual rainfall had fallen in the space of just a few days. As pressures built, threatening the villages in the Arno valley, engineers upstream of Florence made the catastrophic decision to open a dam, unknowingly condemning the city regarded as the cradle of the Renaissance.

The city was completely unprepared. Large parts of the banks of the Arno collapsed. Thirty four thousand people were rescued by emergency services. Five thousand families were rendered homeless and six thousand businesses destroyed. Six hundred thousand tons of mud, rubble and sewage severely damaged and destroyed nearly four million books and manuscripts and fourteen thousand articles of fine art. It took two days for the waters to recede.

Many international governments and organisations would eventually lend aid, but no official help arrived for six days. Pablo Picasso auctioned one of his works for funds. A Franco Zeffirelli documentary raised $20million.

But fondest remembered of all are those who volunteered their services for no pay, the *angeli del fagno* – the 'mud angels'. Some were locals, others travelled for days to be there. No one organised or recruited them. Throughout the winter they continued to arrive from far afield. They slept in railway cars. They brought food and water to elderly Florentines trapped in their apartments. They shovelled mud and carried priceless works of art to safety. They cleaned, dried and treated countless works of art. They were an expression of the internationalist instincts, transnational travel and generational solidarity that had developed out of the new-found postwar mobility of the youth of Western Europe. Florence remains forever indebted to them.

In the aftermath of the disaster, a cohort of over two hundred artists banded together to show solidarity and raise funds for the smitten city. Forty of them were women; they became known as 'the Flood Ladies', and their art remains celebrated in the city to this day.

Chapter 2
Oxford
April 2018

How ironic it was to have both the best thing and the worst thing to ever have happened to you occur simultaneously. Lucrezia sat stupefied in her bedroom, listening to her mother's screams from downstairs, flinching at the crash of yet more smashed crockery.

She flicked open her MacBook and opened the email again, seeking to ground herself once more. From Giulia Bianchi, Head of Art Restoration at the Palazzo Moretti, Lungarno Guicciardini, Firenze. 'Dear Lucrezia. I am delighted to inform you that we have accepted your application, through the University of Oxford, to study on our Art Restoration course, as an exchange student, for the academic year 2018-19. Many congratulations. Further details are included in the attached documentation. I look forward to personally welcoming you in beautiful Florence!'

Despite the ache in her heart, she felt an intense pride and satisfaction at her achievement. Palazzo Moretti was a highly respected seat of learning and would be a feather in her cap when she graduated from Oxford with her degree in Fine Arts. As a devotee of art history, in particular Florentine renaissance and Mannerist art, a trip to the city widely regarded as the birthplace of the Renaissance was a mouthwatering prospect. And yet…

They had been at the morning Easter Sunday service at the University church of Saint Mary the Virgin. All three felt intensely involved in the life of the University, both parents being respected academics and Lucrezia a successful undergraduate and keen participant in student politics. She campaigned for women's rights and equality, speaking out about the glass ceiling that was still evident in academia. As they walked home on a fine spring morning, chatting amiably about the sermon and their plans for the Easter holidays, none of them could have guessed at the chaos about to be unleashed.

It all began with a ring at the front door, answered by her mother as her father was, as usual, entombed in his study, and Lucrezia, basking in the glory of her acceptance in Florence, was composing a triumphant announcement to her proud parents. Then came the first of many screams, the slamming of the front door, her mother bellowing 'Jeffrey!' and her father emerging like a mole from a burrow, blinking in surprise. As Lucrezia reached the upstairs landing, she witnessed the unconscionable; her mother slapping her father across the face and calling him a bastard.

Then they were both speaking simultaneously, fighting to be heard. She, berating him for being unfaithful, deceiving her all these years, destroying their family. He, apologising and saying it was long over, had meant nothing, he loved only her. Two conflicting dramas played out in parallel, making no sense but conveying a sense of unavoidable doom.

As if in a dream, she descended into the maelstrom, striving to make someone, anyone, tell her what the hell was happening.

"Your father's been cheating on me – that was *her* husband warning him to stay away!" yelled her mother.

Her father backed away, hands raised in attempted mitigation. "Marie, I told you, it ended *years* ago. It meant nothing. I love *you*, it's always been *you*."

Her mother, laughing now, verging on hysterical. "Oh, well, that's *okay* then, isn't it? Nothing to see here then! What do *you* think, Lucrezia?"

How to answer a question when your heart is breaking? She ran upstairs, closing the bedroom door, holding her hands over her ears and screwing her eyes tight shut. This isn't happening. Make it go away. The slam of the front door. The car starting, speeding out of the driveway.

She could hear her mother crying downstairs. Summoning the strength to put aside her own pain, she quietly descended to the kitchen, where her mother sat huddled at the table, head in her hands, her body racked with keening sobs. Lucrezia moved softly to her side and embraced her, attempting to share her pain and apply a salve. She had no words; the moment felt too immense to encapsulate in a sentence or two.

And yet, Marie, never one to shirk a challenge, attempted the task using only three letters. Raising her watering eyes and fixing Lucretia with a piteous stare, she mouthed 'Why?'

Lucrezia responded with a shake of her head, a gesture succinctly enfolding her incomprehension. How could she begin to assimilate the demise of her parents' marriage, the immolation of all they had created together over thirty years, the evaporation of three futures in the blink of an eye?

Eleanora di Toledo
Court of Viceroy of Naples, 1535

He is handsome, she thinks. Well built and strong, tall for sixteen, with dark curls above a high forehead and dark, almost black eyes which exude a confidence which is picked up by his retinue. His beard and moustache are a bit straggly perhaps, but there is time for them to develop into a more impressive presence. His dark armour with its ruby red trimmings presents an imposing addition. He strides purposefully forward to face her father, Pedro Alvarez de Toledo, who is standing a respectful pace behind Charles V, and sketches a deep bow, as one must bestow upon a man of the Emperor's standing.

Stepping back, he lets his cousin, Alessandro, take centre stage. He's a strange, ugly man, thinks Eleanora, so swarthy. They say his mother is a negro maidservant. Hardly befitting a man of the heft of the Duke of Florence. Perhaps that's why he so craves the support of the Holy Roman Emperor; it's said that his own citizens are verging on revolt.

She's looking at Cosimo again, and imagines that the faintest of smiles flits across his face. At thirteen she has begun the process of maturation, already of a marriageable age, a fact her father has mentioned on more than one occasion. She has, she thinks, a pretty, round face, with a pert little nose and rosebud lips. The boys in court call her pretty at least, although they tease her that she should smile more. The presence of her elder sister, Isabella, might prove a barrier to her advancement, but her father says that *both* daughters of an important man like the Viceroy of Naples would be attractive proportions to potential suitors and that they can both expect to make matches advantageous to the family position. And yet, there's a stubborn part of her that believes, especially as she's *much* prettier than Isabella, she should be allowed to choose and to marry for love.

Would she choose Cosimo? Well, he *is* a Medici, albeit not from the main branch of the family, or so her mother says. They remain the most powerful family in one of the most influential cities in Italy, and one with whom, even in these times of ever shifting allegiances, the Holy

Roman Emperor and the court of Naples are currently aligned. Their wealth knows no bounds and she has become accustomed to the finer things in life.

But he's a mere page boy at present, and not even in line to take power in the future, should anything happen to Alessandro – an ever present possibility in these turbulent, war-riven times. Who knows what her future holds?

Chapter 3
Oxford
May 2018

It was heartbreaking to see her father so defeated. He sat opposite her in the café, stirring his coffee endlessly, long after the sugar would have dissolved, gazing into the mug as if wishing he could drown in its contents. His thin frame seemed to have receded still further, his round face was pasty, the dark eyes lost in shadow and his lank, dark hair glistened with an oily, unwashed sheen. He hadn't shaved in days, his shirt was stained and, she was mortified to notice, the aroma emanating from his direction suggested a shower was a similar distant memory.

She reached across the table and covered his hand, making him desist from the stirring. He slowly raised his eyes, as if noticing her for the first time, but his gaze passed through her as if she wasn't there.

"You need to snap out of it, dad," she suggested, immediately recognising the fruitlessness of the comment. Reaching for something more helpful, she surfaced with, "Perhaps it would help if you wrote to mum, since she won't take your calls…?"

He was shaking his head long before she finished, acknowledging the futility of the situation. "It's no good, Lu, her mind's made up. You know your mother, she sees the world in black and white. It's game over, no second chances. I've already heard from Andrew, who's been contacted by your mother's solicitor with a view to commencing divorce proceedings. He'll play for time, try to pour oil on troubled waters but he doesn't hold out much hope and I don't blame him." Andrew Pennington was Jeffrey's solicitor, an affable and efficient professional with whom Jeffery had a friendship dating back to their university days.

In her heart, Lucrezia knew he was right. Her mother had always ploughed her own furrow and showed scant regard for opinions which ran contrary to her own. Ironically, this steely determination was one of the qualities that her father most admired in her; now, it seemed, it would forever firmly act against him. It was inconceivable that she would break the habit of a lifetime to accommodate an understanding of her husband's infidelity. To be honest, Lucrezia didn't understand her father's actions either, and she felt she deserved an explanation.

"*Why,* dad? I never imagined that you were seeing someone else. I mean, you never *go* anywhere; you're either in the office at work or your study at home. I practically have to make an appointment to get your attention you're so absorbed in the literary world. When did you find the *time* to have an affair!"

He sighed and drained half his mug of coffee. A strange smile of reminiscence tugged at the corner of his mouth; Lucrezia fought down an urge to slap him. "It was many years ago, and then only for a few months. A fellow English professor. We met up only occasionally when I said I was working late at the University. We both agreed early on that it had been fun but was going nowhere. As for *why*? I think I've forgotten why." He went back to stirring the coffee.

"If you were looking for *fun,* you could have taken up golf, or salsa, and gone with mum. Screwing someone else's wife isn't my definition of a fun pastime. Weren't we enough for you any more?"

He simply looked away and shrugged his shoulders.

Exasperated, Lucrezia slammed her hand down on the table, making adjacent customers jump and tut in disapproval. "Fuck, dad," she hissed, "that's pathetic!"

This time it was with a nod that he pre-empted her comments. "Yes, I agree. I'm pathetic, and now I've got what I deserve."

Stung by his self-pity, Lucrezia went on the offensive. "Where's your self respect gone? You're a published academic, an emeritus professor, admired by students and colleagues alike. You've supported mum and I, emotionally and practically, all my life. I don't pretend to understand why you did what you did, and it's too early to forgive you, but you're still the father I love.

"You need to sort yourself out. I'm leaving for Florence tomorrow and I'm not going to pass a chance like this up. Mum is getting on with her life, picking up the pieces. I suggest you do the same. Where are you staying?"

He looked up, his appearance so crestfallen that she genuinely didn't recognise the man who had hung the moon for her for so many years. The man to whom she had brought all her cares and worries, safe in the knowledge that he would unburden her and put the world to rights. Would her life ever be the same again? "The Crown Hotel."

She pushed her seat away and turned to leave. Over her shoulder, all she could bring herself to say was, "Take care of yourself."

~

Walking home, absorbed in all her misery, Lucrezia was oblivious to the splendour of Oxford's historic centre. Despite having lived here all her life, the majesty of the mustard sandstone colleges normally still stirred a feeling of pride within her. She turned at Carfax tower and headed along The High Street, not noticing the university buildings of Oriel and Magdalen colleges, which loomed over her, solicitous in their attendance. Crossing the road, she entered the shade of the peaceful botanic gardens and headed towards the River Cherwell and the path home.

'Home'! She snorted in suppressed rage at the concept. A place of sanctuary all her adult life, ripped asunder in a cataclysmic moment. Anger consumed her, thrusting out in all directions at once. Her father: how could he have been so deceitful and, now, so naïve? Her mother: why would she not even *listen* to him – surely all the years of love and attention he had bestowed upon her merited at least that much? And the husband of her father's previous love interest: what merit was there in destroying a marriage years after the infidelity had come to an end?

And there was the nub of her difficulties - seeking to solve questions of the heart solely with the head.

Lucrezia was not involved in a relationship. Cerebral rather than passionate, her contact with her peers was consummately academic. She struggled to understand the emotions involved and the inability of both parents to think their way through the crisis.

Even the young men in her year, if asked, would have defined her predominantly in terms of character rather than sentiment: intelligent, with strong feminist views, able to hold her own in a debate and normally tolerant of the views of others, unless perceiving them as chauvinistic. Conventional, playing by the rules and expecting likewise of others. Predictable to the point of stoicism.

A few brave souls looked beyond to the physical, seeing a small, slightly built woman of twenty three, with long permed blonde hair, piercing blue eyes and a pale complexion, who dressed in bohemian style and eschewed make up, possessing a fragile natural beauty. There was something ineffably aloof about Lucrezia; one was encouraged to engage in discussion and debate but sentimentality and tenderness were somehow off limits. She collected friends and acquaintances but required them to orbit at a respectable distance.

Even the great interest in her life, art (others would have called it a passion) was appreciated mainly in intellectual terms. Her knowledge of art history was encyclopaedic; show her a painting and chances were she could rhyme off who painted it, when and where, the current location of the work, other items from the artist's *oeuvre* and a potted biography of the artist – where he was born and died, what artists influenced him, what influence he had on subsequent artists and the historical context in which he lived. Much less likely was that she would tell you whether she actually liked the painting, or how it made her *feel*.

It was the same with her forthcoming trip to Florence and the opportunity to learn about art restoration and conservation. The thrill of having hands on contact with priceless, revered works of art, the pride of being part of their resurrection played second fiddle to an inventory of the techniques and materials to be used.

Little did she know that the weeks ahead would be the most emotionally demanding of her young life.

Chapter 4
Oxford
May 2018

Jeffrey sat opposite Andrew Pennington in his office in the centre of town. Although his friend and lawyer was talking, he was gazing over his right shoulder out the window, where a cat walked precariously along the ridge of a roof. 'I know how he feels,' thought Jeffrey.

"Jeffrey? Did you hear what I said?"

He jerked himself back into the room. "Sorry Andrew, was miles away."

Pennington sighed and put his pen down, reclining in his chair. "I've never seen you so distracted. God knows, if you get your head in a book yes, but we've got to tackle this head on; she's coming at you all guns blazing. You need to take a position and act."

Jeffrey smiled ironically. Two things he found nigh on impossible. He was the master placater, the personification of indolence. 'Things just happen *to me'* was his motto.

"Jeffrey, I'm your best friend, the Watson to your Holmes. Probably your *only* friend. I'll be frank; this harks back to the way you let Jackson walk all over you back when you had the business. You need to defend yourself man!"

Jeffrey's mind drifted back twenty years to the business he had established with his university friend, Jackson Hill. They had established a dealership in rare antiquarian books in Oxford, seeking to utilise the combined knowledge from their degrees – his in English literature and Jackson's in business studies. And for a while it developed precisely along those lines. Jeffrey knew the niche market inside out, what books would sell, where to order from, how to generate academic interest. And Jackson knew how to maximise profit and, more importantly, how to siphon the vast majority of that into his own coffers and how to do so in a manner that, when Jeffrey discovered and challenged him, ensured that he was completely untouchable. At that point, Jackson essentially thumbed his nose and walked away, leaving Jeffrey with a failing business and mounting debts.

Never one to comfortably socialise, Jeffrey became completely isolated, retreating into academia and his marriage. Marie had been simultaneously supportive and disappointed, a blend that inevitably distanced the pair. Brought up by overbearing, expectant parents, Jeffrey had always struggled with self esteem and intimacy and Marie was a bustling, efficient woman who rarely took time to embrace the sensitive side of her nature. With Lucrezia growing into a charming, bright child, they lived their emotional lives vicariously through her imagination and ploughed on in their separate academic furrows.

Lucrezia was ten when Jeffrey became involved with Linda. It wasn't about sex (well, not *just* about sex) he told himself. She was attentive, she listened and cared. He could open up to her, tell her about his hopes, dreams and fears and always she *listened*; she didn't look at her watch, or interrupt, as Marie did when he tried to engage her. Growing emotionally close seemed to lead naturally to physical intimacy and the sex had been good – inventive, exciting in its forbidden secrecy. Neither party had ever intended to leave their partners and the decision that the affair had run its natural course was mutual and genial. Jeffrey had no idea why, thirteen years later, her husband had descended on his marital home to deal a crushing, perhaps terminal blow.
"I'm worried about you, Jeffrey." Andrew's words pulled him back to the present. "You've no friends, no fight, a belly full of shame and you're living in a cheap hotel room. You're precisely the type of man who's found dead with a note."

"You always did bolster my spirits, Andrew. What would I do without your support?"

Pennington smiled, glad to see any response from his deflated friend. "I know Marie. She's going to come at you like the Furies from Hades. She'll demand her pound of flesh."

Jeffrey smiled; his friend had a penchant for literary metaphors that were often confusing in their dissonance. "What do you suggest we do?"

"I suggest we refute any petition for divorce. Adopt a position of penitence and contrition. That will both open the door for a possible reconciliation when the temperature has dropped a few degrees and perhaps offset the cost of settling if she pursues despite our best efforts. How's Lucrezia coping with this?"

Jeffrey felt a pang of guilt. "She's devastated of course. The fact that we never argue meant it came as a complete shock to her. She's just been accepted to study in Florence for a year, which is probably the best thing for her right now. Get away and fill her head with beauty and art."

"You should remember that too, Jeffrey. There's beauty to be found in the everyday things. Don't lose hope; better times lie ahead."

Jeffrey smiled accommodatingly; he didn't believe a word of that. He had never been a man of great ambition. Having a book published had been the summit of his aspiration; he felt immensely proud the day that his dissection of the poems of John Donne came out, but chastened by how few copies it eventually sold. To him, there was a perverse inverse relationship between how intellectually valuable something was and how highly merited by society it was. He had come to despise the vacuous, facile, celebrity obsessed world that the young seemed determined to create for themselves and inflict upon everyone else.

No, no beauty in everyday things. And precious little hope.

Eleanora di Toledo
Court of Viceroy of Naples, March, 1539

She always feels anxious when her father summons her. He is a kind
and loving father, quick to praise her and slow to anger, but his role as
Viceroy is demanding, dancing to the tune of the sometimes mercurial
Emperor. On approaching the viceregal apartments she was passed, and
nearly knocked to the floor, by a scowling Isabella, who glared fiercely
at her. What on earth had so upset her sister?

As she timidly knocks and enters the chambers, she is reassured to find
her mother present, who bestows a benevolent smile upon her. "Come
and sit by me, child," she gestures, patting the cushions on the window
seat. As Eleanora settles in beside her, her mother takes her hand and
gently squeezes it, as if to embolden her. It is less than a year since she
brought her children to court and, to her joy, the move has already
borne fruit.

Her father looks up from behind his desk and rises, coming round to
stand before her. She is struck, not for the first time, by how imposing a
figure he cuts in his ceremonial robes. Tall and magisterial, even now
bearing his sword at his side, he at times cuts a distant figure. But not
today. Today, he kneels down before her, an unusual gesture for him,
and gently begins to speak.

"Child, something wonderful has happened. Cosimo de'Medici has
asked for your hand in marriage. You have been invited to join one of
Europe's most prominent families. Isn't this wonderful – such an
honour for you and our family!"

Eleanora is puzzled. "But, father, surely the honour should go to
Isabella?"

Her father looks away for a moment; was he trying not to smile? "Yes,
my child, that was the proposition put to us by the Holy Roman
Emperor, for it was he who arranged this wonderful betrothal. But, em,
Cosimo declined the offer of Isabella's hand. He also declined the offer

of marriage to Vittoria Farnese, none other than the grand daughter of our Holy Father in Rome. It appears it was *you* he remembers from his visit here with Duke Alessandro four years ago. You made quite the impression, young lady." At that, to her astonishment, he bows low before her, making both Eleanora and her mother giggle.

Her mother speaks next. "You are to be married by proxy later this month. Then, in June, you shall set sail for Livorno, thence overland to Pisa and on to Florence. Cosimo will meet you en route and you shall enter Florence in triumph, to the acclaim of all. You will be formally wed in the church of San Lorenzo before June is out. We are both so very proud of you, child."

~

That night, Eleanora is too excited to sleep. She will miss her parents, but the formal stuffiness of the viceregal court has become rather boring and restrictive. She lies imaging her new life with her handsome, powerful, rich husband, waited on as the lady of the house – no, of the *Palazzo* no less! What riches await her; clothes sewn with silver and gold, jewellery of unimaginable splendour, horses and hawks at the country villa of Poggio a Caiano. She is becoming a *Medici*, a daughter of the pre-eminent house of Florence, renown as a centre of artistic excellence and humanist learning. The court here in Naples is woefully lacking in talented artists and writers and she looks forward to broadening her exposure to, and knowledge of, the humanities.

But lurking behind the excitement of a new chapter in her life lies the responsibilities of becoming a wife and mother. Her own mother has carefully laid forth the facts regarding the duties expected of a woman on her wedding night and beyond, attempting to couch the process in more reassuring terms than the whispered miseries and agonies conjured up by the youngsters at court. However, there is no disguising the genuine risks associated with childbirth and she suppresses a shiver which accompanies the prospect of growing to womanhood more precipitously than she had imagined when she awoke that morning.

Chapter 5
Florence
May 2018

There was a reverential atmosphere in the old refectory in the basilica of Santa Croce. Even though the space was busy with tourists, the soaring vaults absorbed the chatter of voices and, adjacent to the large painting of 'The Last Supper', executed by Giorgio Vasari in 1546, viewers stood or sat largely in awed silence.

The massive work, eight by twenty one feet and painted on five massive poplar panels, hung on the wall, supported by two winches which could raise it to safety in the event of a flood. This was no mere flight of fancy; the work had gone back on display a mere two years previously following extensive restoration after being damaged by the catastrophic flood which had devastated the basilica, along with much of the city, in 1966.

Lucrezia sat mesmerised in front of the work, taking in its glowing colours and the somewhat affected poses of Jesus and his disciples. Although Vasari represented an important bridge between the High Renaissance and her beloved Mannerist period, he was far from being her favourite artist; like many, she placed his importance in terms of his seminal 'Lives of the Artists' rather than his abilities as a painter.

But this work was symbolic of Florence's determination to overcome the devastation wreaked upon her over fifty years previously. It had taken until 2010 for the Opificio delle Pietre Dure, the organisation who oversees the restoration of art treasures in Florence, to secure funding from the Getty Foundation for a project to restore the work from its damaged state. Only after three years painstaking reconstruction of the timber frame and reassembly of the poplar panels could the painted surface be restored to its former glory. The completed work was testament to the skills and determination of all involved.

These were among the skills which she had come to Florence to assimilate, and here in the basilica she had the amazing opportunity to witness those skills being applied in front of her very eyes. She wandered back into the nave of the main church, marvelling once again at its vast dimensions and the veritable treasure trove of art contained therein. On the right hand wall adjacent to the façade stands the Buonarroti chapel, containing a marble tomb to the peerless Michaelangelo and an adjacent altarpiece, with the painting 'Christ Carrying the Cross', again painted by Vasari, between 1568 and 1572. But the canvas no longer hung in its frame; now it was laid horizontal in front of the altar, suspended in a complex frame of supports around which a team of restorers worked in awed silence. A crowd had gathered to watch their labours, fascinated by the opportunity to witness the miracle of art restoration first hand.

Lucrezia read the accompanying display boards, learning that the Opera di Santa Croce had raised €121,000 from one hundred and thirty two donors in fourteen countries for a project taking fifteen months which was now at the midway stage. Fascinated, she strained through the crowd to reach the front, where she could witness the restorers using focused lights and magnifiers to painstakingly remove the centuries of grime and yellow varnish obscuring the colours of the paint below. In some areas, that paint had cracked and bubbled due to immersion in the 1966 flood; here, the craftsmen chipped away damaged paint flakes and with infinite patience applied matching pigments.

Lucrezia stood for an hour, time slipping past unnoticed as she marvelled at the technique and forbearance of the team. She was thrilled to realise that soon she would have the opportunity to acquire similar attributes. Dreaming of such times, she slipped out of the basilica and made her way home.

~

It was a short walk to the Santo Spirito area where Lucrezia's apartment was located. As she was still revelling in the beauty of the centre of Florence, she walked first along Borgo dei Greci to the Piazza della Signoria, emerging into the square over which towered the magnificent Palazzo Vecchio. The symbol of Florentine power and government presented a formidable façade, its immense crenellations and *campanile* exerting a medieval hold over the heart of the Renaissance city.

Crossing the piazza, she took a left turn and immediately came to the Ponte Vecchio, with its jewellers' shops flanking each side. Mingling with the crowds of tourists window shopping, she sauntered to the middle of the bridge, pausing on the right hand side where a break in the shops, guarded by a statue of the goldsmith Benvenuto Cellini, afforded her a view of the Arno, downstream to the Ponte Santa Trinita. Beyond, to the left, in the *oltrarno* district was Lungarno Giucciardini, where the Palazzo Moretti, in which she would be studying for a year, was located. Behind lay the district of Santo Spirito, whose church and square of that name provided the spiritual heart of the neighbourhood and the location of Lucrezia's charming apartment.

Lucrezia crossed the Ponte Vecchio and turned right along one of the narrow streets with tall buildings which characterised this artisans' quarter. Immediately she was enchanted by the sights, sounds and smells of life in residential Florence. Open fronted shops revealed leather workers stretching, cutting and working hides. The smell of leather and the sounds of hammering evoked the means by which the bags and shoes on display were brought into being. Small shop fronts displayed mouth watering fruits and vegetables, huge crimson tomatoes, swollen purple aubergines, glistening bunches of grapes around which buzzed hungry wasps, adding their sounds to the hubbub of voices which echoed in the streets and lanes of the *oltrarno*. It seemed everyone talked at once and enforced their opinions with gesticulations and facial contortions; this was the real city of the workers and residents of Florence.

Soon, Lucrezia was spilled out into the peace and calm of Piazza di Santo Spirito. The cafes surrounding the square were quiet, with as many locals as tourists enjoying an evening drink, sheltering in the shade of the trees lining the pavements. The fountain in the centre of the piazza gurgled quietly, providing a drink and bath to some local pigeons. The plain façade of the church reflected the sunlight as the sun set over the hills of Florence, the delicate *campanile* providing a jewel-like contrast.

She turned to face the imposing Palazzo Guadagni on the corner of the square. The open loggia on the top had been the first ever built in the city. Her apartment was around the corner from the square here, entered by a small green door and reached by a winding spiral staircase. Although it was compact and didn't have much of a view, she already felt at home here, living as a local while her Florentine adventure got underway.

She stopped at a café and ordered an Aperol spritz, sitting checking her messages as she waited. There was nothing from either of her parents; she imagined them both entrenched in their positions – her mother the betrayed wife and her father the shamed lothario. His position continued to frustrate and worry her; he appeared so accepting of his dismissal, as if his family weren't worth fighting for. She was twenty three now, but being single and still living at home resulted in her family being a bigger part of her life than for many young people her age. The shock of its disintegration was made all the more acute by the fact that her parents never argued or disagreed; perhaps it was the corrosive effects of apathy that had eaten away at the foundations.

Lucrezia secretly hoped she might meet someone while she was in Florence. She would be surrounded by like minded people from all over Europe and beyond, in a beautiful city with romantic connotations. She struggled with intimacy, both emotionally and physically and hoped, rather naively she feared, that a compassionate, similarly shy, fellow student might see beyond the rather prickly façade she often presented and find a way into her heart. Not for the first time, she wished that love was something you could assimilate through reading or tutorials, rather than an emotion which came and went at best irrationally and, at times, completely unbidden.

She had only been in love once before, five years ago as she finished her schooling. He had been her tutor in a summer school she had taken as part of her preparation for university life, older than her by eight years, a brilliant man with a big heart and the capacity to inspire dreams. For the first time, her dreams included attachment and commitment, a life lived in harmonious partnership; sadly, her mentor had a different agenda. His seductive attentions evaporated soon after he deflowered her, an approach which she subsequently found, to her shame, was his normal *modus operandi*. The tenuous filaments with which she had begun to build bridges to people around her were violently sundered and she retreated into a hermetic existence founded on self sufficiency.

People often asked Lucrezia, 'why art?' Sometimes it was out of genuine curiosity, but often, as with so much of what we say, the question fronted an agenda. 'You're so smart, you could do anything. Why not study something *useful*?' was the subtext. As with all really meaningful questions, this was one that Lucrezia had often asked herself. Clearly she had been influenced by her upbringing; both parents were academics in the sphere of the arts, rather than the sciences, to the extent that even her name owed a debt to her mother's passion for Italian history; she had picked the name based on her admiration of Lucrezia Tornabuoni, wife of Piero di Cosimo de' Medici and mother of Lorenzo 'Il Magnifico'.

But she knew that the main reason, the purpose for which art was crafted in her life, was that it offered a way to really give birth to her emotions. Yes, she found the knowledge associated with art – the historical background, the insight into faith and religion, the technical innovations it birthed – fascinating, but looking at art initiated an emotional response of a depth and magnitude that she found she had no other means to access. But at that point, the block set in; she could *feel* it inside but never channel it to the outside, never share it with anyone else.

All that was left was to find a way to nurture that response and grow her emotional intelligence alongside her intellect. Surely Florence was the ideal place to begin?

Eleanora di Toledo
Medici Palace
Florence, 29th June, 1539

Eleanora lies in her nuptial bed in the Medici palace, the curtains drawn around the bed frame. Her ladies in waiting have retired for the night. She awaits, with some trepidation, the arrival of her husband and the consummation of her marriage, the final act in what has been an extraordinary few days.

Finally becoming a woman holds few fears, in truth; she has come to trust and respect Cosimo, almost from the first time they met, on the road between Pisa and Florence, less than a week ago. She had docked at Livorno, having set sail from Naples eleven days previously, accompanied by her brother Garcia and seven galleys of Spanish nobility and servants. The day she set sail had been Cosimo's twentieth birthday – surely an auspicious sign! She was welcomed in Livorno by the Archbishop of Pisa and that very day met Cosimo on the road. They had spent three days in Pisa, visiting local towns, gaining her husband-to-be the favour of the smaller cities in his duchy.

Four days at the Medici villa at Poggio a Caiano had given some welcome respite from her travels. She had spent little time in the country in her young life and revelled in the fresh air, the magnificent Tuscan scenery, the chance to take bucolic walks on the arm of her husband-to-be as they became acquainted. From the moment of their proxy marriage three months previously, they had struck up a correspondence, which quickly became intimate. He had professed his love and admiration, holding forth promises of fidelity and respect. He loudly applauded her attempts to learn and communicate in Italian, the language birthed by the beloved son of Florence, Dante Alighieri. She was very proud of her Spanish heritage but simultaneously wanted to earn the love and respect, not only of her husband, but also of the citizens of her new duchy.

She had finally reached the gates of Florence two days previously, finding a city desperate to celebrate a new dawn in their history under

Grand Duke Cosimo. He had hand picked a new cultural and artistic community for Florence, recruiting painters, architects, poets, playwrights, musicians and courtiers, to evoke the image of Dante, Beatrice and Florence's golden age, as described in *Paradiso*. Florence was one of the most turbulent city states in Europe, plunging between life as a republic and rule under the Medici. The family had resumed control of the city following an eleven month siege in 1531 and their position had only been consolidated when Pope Clement VII, himself a Medici, appointed Florence a Grand Duchy, with Alessandro as its head.

The city had been bedecked in splendour under the watchful eye of the artist il Tribolo, who had erected a welcome arch at the gate; columns, pilasters, cornices and pediments full of countless scenes and figures, the most prominent being a female in ancient dress representing Fecundity. She was flanked by Security and Eternity, standing upon Time and surrounded by depictions of the Medici victorious in battle.

In rode Eleanora, wearing crimson satin embroidered with gold thread, set off with a gold coif around her neck and a diamond ring, wedding gifts from Cosimo. Artillery fire from the Spanish troops at the Fortezza da Basso was accompanied by shouts of praise from the cheering crowds and by tributes from musicians and singers who, flanking the gate, lauded her with a newly composed eight part ceremonial motet.

She was paraded through the streets to the cathedral of Santa Maria del Fiore and welcomed by Archbishop Buondelmonti, before being escorted to the Medici palace.There, the decorations were even more sumptuous; Bronzino had excelled himself with depictions of Medici triumphs including Leo X entering Florence and Clement VII blessing the Holy Roman Emperor Charles V. Paintings showed scenes from the lives of the Medici with inscriptions from antiquity, and there was an image of Charles V depicted as Caesar Augustus. Central to the decorative scheme were the coats of arms of the two families about to be united, embraced by the double headed eagle, the Hapsburg emblem of Charles, emphasising Cosimo's strong pro-imperial sentiment.

But Cosimo was also looking to the future as well as celebrating the past. A new image appeared, one of an old, bent and broken laurel, with a new shoot emerging from the stump and the motto *uno avulso,* alluding to the succession of Cosimo after the assassination of Alessandro and the rise of the new branch of the Medici.

~

That morning, Eleanora had dressed under the attention of her ladies in waiting. Her dress of ivory satin shot through with threads of gold and silver had a tight fitting bodice with puffed sleeves, and a fuller skirt, whose central panel in gold brocade was embroidered with the Florentine lily. Her hair was bound in a jewel encrusted circlet. Looking in the mirror she had been pleased with her appearance and hoped her husband would find her equally appealing.

He had cut a dashing figure when he arrived to escort her the short distance to the church of San Lorenzo. As a sign of respect to the origins of Charles, Cosimo had dressed in Spanish style, in black velvet doublet and hose, his doublet trimmed with gold brocade and ermine. He carried his sword and bowed low in respect for his bride to be, receiving a shy smile in reply.

Together they entered the church, passing though the unadorned façade into the interior, designed in the previous century by Filippo Brunelleschi. Grey stone columns stretched the length of the nave, receding in the perfect harmony beloved of the famous architect. From their beautiful capitals, arches reached heavenwards, culminating in a magnificent white coffered ceiling. They promenaded towards the high altar, witnessed by nobles from Florence and beyond, passing between Donatello's twin pulpits and blessed by Fra Filippo Lippi's glorious 'Annunciation' in the north transept. Eleanora baulked slightly at being the centre of attention for so many watchful eyes, reassured by the stout presence of her partner. Cosimo felt the presence of his dynasty all around; this was, after all, the Medici family church. To his left he could see Verocchio's marble, porphyry and bronze memorial to Piero and Giovanni. And, as he stopped by the high altar, in front of the priest who bestowed the benediction upon them, he knew that, beneath his feet, was the tomb of the founder of the dynasty, Cosimo il Vecchio, who had died in 1464.

The wedding banquet was both a sensory delight and a political statement. Course after course was presented to the enthralled guests with unequalled style and panache. Men sat on one side of the banqueting hall and women on the other. The wine flowed freely. The plates were from Venice, made of copper with enamel and gold. Chickens, ducks and other small birds were followed by saltwater seafood and silver-scaled fish from the Arno. Lard, sausage and tongue. As centrepiece, an entire peacock had been cooked, recomposed and then the feathers added back. The Medici palace had been sculpted entirely from spun sugar. Baskets full of sweetmeats, tarts and pomegranates ended the meal.

The whole wedding day had been designed to present their subjects and rivals with an effective reminder of Florence's cultural superiority and power. The assembled nobles from Florence and abroad were left in no doubt regarding the magnificence of the Medici household. The events were chronicled, documented and reported to other heads of state.

After the sumptuous banquet, there were musical tributes from Pisa, Volterra, Arrezzo, Cortona, Pistoia and Rome. A play by Antonio Landi was performed, set in a recreation of the city of Pisa. Apollo appeared, dressed in crimson taffeta, lyre in one hand, bow in the other, wearing a green laurel crown and singing of union and rebirth.

~

As the guests drift away, cognisant of the final chapter to be played out between bride and groom, Eleanora looks forward to her new life as First Lady of Florence. With the final inebriated farewells, the *Palazzo* grows quiet. She hears the footsteps of her husband, ascending the stairs to the bridal room. The door opens quietly; although he has caroused and drunk his share of wine with his guests, Cosimo is a man who chooses to remain in control at all times and has, from the beginning, proven himself sensitive to the wishes of his bride. Inadvertently, she pulls the sheet higher over her chest, a gesture which elicits a smile from the Duke.

"So shy, my love? I trust the thought of our sharing the marital bed does not alarm you?"

She smiles back. "Not so, my husband. You have shown yourself full of care and love for my needs. I am grateful to you for that."

He frowns, puzzled. "It is no more than that to which you are entitled. You are my wife and to you my love and devotion will be singular and eternal. I intend to rule my duchy with great pride and I will fight to preserve that which has been given to me, but I am no despot nor tyrant and will endeavour to be fair and wise. These are qualities I have found in you and I ask you to rule by my side and to build a dynasty with me, blessed with many children. In return, I pledge to you my lifelong fidelity and companionship."

He has been undressing as he speaks and now removes his shift, standing naked before her. It is not only his magnificent physique that stirs her; his words ring true and her admiration and desire form a heady brew. She pulls down the sheet, revealing her nakedness to him, and gestures for him to join her in bed.

Chapter 6
Florence
May 2018

Lucrezia walked the short distance from her apartment to the Palazzo Moretti, feeling a mixture of excitement and apprehension. It was the first day of her attachment to the institute and, while looking forward to starting her studies, she was cognisant that her classmates already knew each other and fearful that her rather limited grasp of Italian might inhibit her making friends. She needn't have worried.

The façade of the sixteenth century Palazzo was magnificent. In keeping with other buildings of the time, the façade presented three levels; the lowest gave an impression of fortification, with rustic blocks, imposing square windows and inlaid ironwork, designed for tethering horses and inserting torches. The middle floor was more refined, the stonework smoother and the windows taking on the bifora style, with rounded arches. This refinement was even more marked on the upper floor, which was finished in Ashlar stone and topped by an impressive overhanging cornice. Through a central doorway one reached an majestic internal courtyard, home to some modern style sculpture and the main student entrance, through which Lucrezia strode in expectation.

Internally, she was surprised to find, the building had a distinctly contemporary look, finished in tinted glass and steel, open plan offices and workspaces, with a light, airy feel. The signage was in both Italian and English; as bidden, she presented herself at reception and asked for Giulia Bianchi, the professor of art restoration who was to be her mentor. After just a few moments, Giulia appeared, the epitome of Italian style and beauty. Olive skinned with dark hair cut in a bob, with high cheekbones and stunning green eyes, she sported designer sunglasses perched above her brow. She wore a figure hugging green dress, exquisitely cut; Lucretia was no fashionista but could tell it was designer. Her shapely legs were enhanced by high heel shoes, again clearly high end. She had a cream jacket casually slung over one shoulder, effortlessly chic. Face wearing the broadest of smiles, arms outstretched, she glided over to embrace Lucrezia, kissing her lightly on each cheek.

"*Cara mia, benvenuto.* Welcome to Palazzo Moretti. We're thrilled to have you join us," she cooed.

Lucrezia laughed, enchanted by the warmth of her welcome. "Thank you *so* much! I'm overjoyed to be here. Florence is even more beautiful than I had imagined."

Giulia beamed, pleased by this affirmation of her beloved city. "Wait until you've lived here a few months and Firenze has adopted you as her daughter. To live here is to know true beauty and joy. Please, come into my office and we can begin to orientate you to our curriculum."

Lucrezia followed Giulia into a magnificent office with views of the Arno and took a seat opposite the desk. As Giulia powered up her computer, Lucrezia caught sight of a large print hanging on the wall. It was clearly a representation of the Last Supper, but not one she recognised. "That's an interesting painting," she commented, "I don't recognise the artist."

Giulia looked up from the screen, beaming. "It's by Plautilla Nelli – have you heard of her?"

Lucrezia shook her head. "No, I'm interested in women artists but she's a new name to me. Was she Florentine?"

"Yes, she was born in San Felipe but entered a convent at fourteen. She became prioress at one time, under the auspices of the Dominicans and Savonarola. Believe it or not, she was entirely self taught; she learned by copying the works of Bronzino, del Sarto and Fra Bartolommeo. She even got a mention in Vasari's 'Lives', although 'so many pictures that it would be tedious to attempt to speak of them all' is hardly his most comprehensive depiction. It seems chauvinism was alive even then." She smiled to inject humour into her barb.

Lucrezia had been studying the work, struck by the contrast between the luminous colours of the disciples' clothes and the white linen tablecloth, and strangely moved by the passionate if somewhat stylised emotions on the faces and in the gestures of the ensemble cast. "Where is the painting; I can't tell if it's a fresco or panel?"

"It's a canvas, a large one too; seven metres by two metres. At the moment we're restoring it from a fairly precarious state. It had been taken out of its frame and stored rolled up, causing extensive damage. The organisation of which I'm part, Advancing Women Artists, is working on it in our conservation studios. It's a four year project and we're over half way there. I can take you to see it, if you'd like?"

"That would be *wonderful*, thank you!" beamed Lucrezia. "I intend to seek out as much work by women artists as I can while I'm here, but I'm only really familiar with Artemisia Gentileschi."

"Well, now you know Plautilla too. We have lectures on women artists during our course and I'm happy to provide you with lists of where you can see their works here in Florence."

She made several keyboard entries in silence. Lucrezia exercised her curiosity. "Have you worked her for long?"

Giulia smiled at her. "A few years. I studied art history in Milan and then spent several years working in fashion design. But my heart was never really in it - it's a very cutthroat business. Fortunately, a mutual acquaintance put me in touch with Tommaso Rialo who was looking for someone to head up the institute here. He was generous enough to fund the training I required to be fully equipped for the role and keep it open for me while I studied."

Lucrezia reflected on how generous an offer that represented and looked forward to seeing if Tommaso really was that philanthropic.

Guilia rose to retrieve some papers she had printed off and handed them to Lucrezia with a smile. "Here is a timetable of lectures and seminars you can attend. It's entirely up to you to pick and choose what content most interests you. I'll be liaising with Oxford to assure you of our best attention in meeting your requirements while you're here. Now, why don't I show you the cafeteria and you can meet some of your new classmates?"

Lucrezia followed her along the corridor and upstairs, emerging on a rooftop terrace, partly covered and with an open air seating area affording magnificent views across the Arno to the main heart of the city. The café was about half full, some students eating and drinking, alone or in groups, some working on laptops or simply enjoying the sunshine and the panorama.
Giulia headed towards a large table around which sat a group of students, engaged in a discussion, with notes laid out in front of them. They greeted her cheerily, pulling out chairs for her and Lucrezia. She raised a hand in greeting. "Thank you but I'm not staying. I'd like to introduce you to Lucrezia; she's here on a year long exchange from Oxford and will be attending classes with you. Can I leave you to introduce yourselves and tell her a little about what you're studying?" They chorused their approval and, with a reassuring hand on Lucrezia's shoulder, Giulia left.

One by one the group welcomed her and introduced themselves – Anna, Laura, Sofia, Stefano and Gio. Anna, who seemed to be the appointed chairperson, told her they were preparing an essay on the Mannerist artist Jacopo Pontormo and his recently restored work, 'The Deposition from the Cross', which had just been returned to the altar of the Capponi chapel in the nearby church of Santa Felicita. She showed Lucrezia a print of the altarpiece. "Have you seen it yet – it's magnificent!"

Lucrezia shook her head, instantly liking this bubbly, attractive girl who smiled easily in welcome. "No, it's a new one on me."

"We'll take you," suggested Sofia, a tall, swarthy girl, wearing sunglasses and exuding style and confidence. "It's only a few minutes from here."

"How are you liking Florence?" asked Stefano, pulling a packet of cigarettes from his jacket and offering them to Lucrezia.

"I love it, it's even more spectacular than I had dreamed," said Lucrezia, waving away the offer.

Gio grabbed the packet, playfully. "Put it away, Stef, we don't want you fouling up our beautiful air!" He winked at Lucrezia. He's a flirt, she thought, but when you look that good, you can pull it off. Even seated, she could tell Gio was tall; add in athletic and ruggedly handsome. He wore designer denims and a tight fitting tee shirt, making the most of his physique. His dark hair was worn in a pony tail, and his handsome face was enhanced by a trim moustache and sunglasses. Even though she knew his game, Lucrezia considered that it might be one she would be willing to play.

"Why don't I grab some lunch and listen while you finish your discussion?" suggested Lucrezia, rising to head to the counter. Soon she returned with a sandwich and soft drink and tuned in to the group discussion. It was evident that there was much excitement about the restoration work in Santa Felicita, not just about the altarpiece, widely regarded as Pontormo's masterpiece, but about the chapel itself. The chapel had been built by Brunelleschi at the same time as he was working on his seminal Ospedale degli Innocenti. Pontormo had also frescoed an 'Annunciation' flanking an external window, and three Evangelists in the pendentives. The fourth pendentive contained a fresco of St. Mark by Agnolo Bronzino.

Restoration had taken a year, under the supervision of Daniele Rossi, and been funded by the Friends of Florence, thanks to the patronage of Kathe and John Dyson. The fact that private sponsorship had been required had reignited the debate about whether the Italian state was doing enough to support the arts. It was this subject that the students had been tasked to debate in their submissions and there was a heated venting of opinions underway when Lucrezia excused herself and went to explore the rest of the Palazzo.

Thirty minutes later she left and noticed Gio, across the street, perched on the wall overlooking the Arno, casually smoking. He raised an arm in salute and gestured her over. Had he been waiting for her? Not wanting to be rude, she waved back and crossed to meet him, relieved to see him flick his cigarette into the river. "Hi," he said, "I wondered if you would like to see Santa Felicita? I'd love to see it again myself."

"Sure, that would be lovely, thank you."

He gestured for her to walk and casually slipped in alongside her, his leather jacket slung over his shoulder. Despite him being a smoker, the aroma he gave off was of a musky, expensive cologne. Together they strolled along the *lungarno* and within minutes stood outside a tiny, unprepossessing church. Gio entered first, holding the door for Lucrezia, who paused inside to allow her eyes to adjust to the light.

Immediately inside the church on the right was the most beautiful painting she had ever seen. Her eyes flitted over its magnificent surface, absorbing the luminous colours, pinks and blues predominantly, the sinuous movements of the figures, the pathos of the attendants taking the dead Christ down from the cross and bearing witness to his Passion. The work was contained within a magnificent gilt frame and shone as if lit from within. Lucrezia felt an intense wave of emotion, of joy that man could create such beauty and gratitude that she was blessed enough to be able to stand before it in adulation, as so many had before her. The atmosphere was reverential, those assembled stood in awed, respectful silence. She caught the gaze of a wizened, hunched old man, tears in his eyes, who nodded his understanding and fellowship to her.

Normally, Lucrezia approached art through knowledge and understanding, aware of who had commissioned the work, by whom and when it was painted, what techniques had been employed, what had influenced the artist and what influence this work had had on those who followed. Art history was her passion and she had accrued a significant knowledge across many art movements. The Mannerists, including Pontormo, were among the groups she had studied, and she was aware of his oeuvre and associations with contemporaries. But, even if she had no knowledge of art history whatsoever, she could have appreciated the sheer aesthetic beauty of what was displayed before her. She knew she would return to worship this painting over and over again, and counted herself blessed to be living only minutes from this church.

Gio had stepped outside and was waiting when she emerged blinking into the evening light.
He smiled to see her expression. "It's quite something isn't it?"

"Oh Gio, it's the most beautiful thing I've ever seen. I was moved to tears, words are inadequate to convey my feelings right now."

He gently squeezed her arm; she was aware but did not react. "I'm glad you liked it. Can I walk you home?"

"No, no, I'm literally round the corner. Thank you so much for bringing me here!"

He took off his sunglasses and flashed her a dazzling smile. "It was my very great pleasure. I hope I will see you at the Palazzo tomorrow. By the way, my father, who is a patron of the institute, is holding a party there on Saturday evening – I very much hope you will attend?"

She smiled in return and raised a hand in farewell. "Yes, thank you I shall. See you tomorrow."

Eleanora di Toledo
Poggio a Caiano, 1541

She loves their visits to the country. The villa at Poggio a Caiano is her favourite place to spend time out of the city. From the moment the carriage pulls up at the entrance and she and Cosimo ascend the sweeping staircase to the entrance, the views over the surrounding *campagna* soothe her soul. As the servants bustle about, taking their belongings into the porticoed basement, she gazes out at the farmlands they own. From the villa's position on top of a natural hill, the vistas are virtually endless, perhaps limited by a shimmer of heat haze, a hint of *sfumato* on the horizon. Entering the villa is like entering an ancient temple, passing below the glorious terracotta frieze and between the pilasters.

She is pregnant with their second child. Baby Maria will soon celebrate her first birthday; she is a happy, amiable child who smiles easily, as if already conscious of the life with which she has been blessed. Eleanora hopes that she will present Cosimo with a son this time – any child is a gift from God, but she knows how much, like any ruler, he craves a male heir.

Cosimo seems more relaxed here too. Sometimes the responsibility of rule weighs heavy on his shoulders; Eleanora is one of the few who can calm Cosimo in his anger or soften his heart to forgiveness. He is not quick to anger, but she can sense his frustration early, often merely from the set of his jaw, and the simple act of gently touching his arm is enough to bring a smile back to his face. Being her with her seems to *centre* him somehow.

It would be difficult not to feel a sense of dynastic pride here, surrounded by the labours of his illustrious predecessors. Lorenzo himself had been the catalyst, engaging Giuliano da Sangallo to shape the old farmhouse which once stood here into a residence fit for Florence's foremost family. But the defining moment came under Giovanni, elected Pope as Leo the tenth, who crafted the crowning glory of the villa, its central hall. The magnificent stuccoed ceiling is richly gilded and centred on the Medici coat of arms, surmounted by the Papal keys and crown. Cosimo can often be seen standing in the centre of the hall, gazing up at this symbol of supremacy, basking in its reflected glory. Eleanora, to whom beauty is a more comfortable companion than power, prefers to gaze upon the walls, frescoed so beautifully by *Signores* Pontormo, del Sarto and Franciabigio.

~

That evening, the weather is fair and Eleanora strolls alone through the farmlands to where her bees in their hives buzz industriously. She rarely has time alone; even in her chambers in the Palazzo Vecchio her retinue of Spanish courtiers dance attendance upon her, rather like the bees who surround her now. The workers on the farm have built the hives from the wood of the native fig trees, which they then coat with a mixture of ash and cow dung. Soon it will be time to harvest the honey; they will drive the bees out to pasture, using smoke from dried cow dung, remove the combs and then sweep out the hives for the swarms' return. She will soon enjoy the sweet taste of honey eaten from the comb.

She wanders happily among the grove of mulberry trees towards the rooms where the silk is produced. Racks of shelves hold silkworms, chewing away on the mulberry leaves provided. Branches from the trees, on which the worms form their cocoons, are propped up against the far wall. The cocoons will be harvested and dissolved in boiling water, from where the individual fibres will be extracted and fed into the spinning reel. She, personally, has been a major driving force behind the burgeoning silk industry in Florence, generating the beautiful material from which the brocade is woven to manufacture the dresses in her collection. There has been a noticeable shift away from the previously profitable wool industry. Skilled labourers have flocked to the city from Venice, Genoa and Lucca. It has helped, of course, that Cosimo had passed a decree prohibiting silk manufacturing in other cities in the duchy. Money attracts money, as it always has and always will, and some of the city's wealthiest citizens have transferred sums of capital to the growing silk trade and even set up gold beating companies to feed the production of gold thread and leaf for the new fabrics. The industry is now one of the most prosperous in Europe, selling cloth in Naples, Rome, Valencia, Bruges, London and Constantinople. Eleanora is proud that she has now established herself as a woman of independent means, no longer merely dependent on her husband for the finer things in life which she enjoys.

Her independence means much to Eleanora. She loves both her parents with all her heart, but theirs is the traditional relationship where the woman is subservient to the needs of her husband. Her mother does not appear begrudging of this arrangement and her father treats her lovingly and well, but Eleanora would never be content to be defined merely in terms of her relationship to her husband. She is still so very young, but she believes in her heart that she can leave her own mark on the world.

Chapter 7
Florence
May 2018

As Lucrezia checked her emails that morning, she found one from Giulia, subject 'visit today'. Curious, she flicked it open as she drank her second espresso at the café in the piazza.

'*Buongiorno*! Today I am taking a group into the Palazzo Vecchio to the apartments of Eleanora di Toledo. They are closed to the public in preparation for *restauro*. Please join us! We are meeting at the equestrian statue in Piazza della Signoria at midday'.

Lucrezia smiled at the warmth of the message and the thought behind the gesture. It was another wonderful opportunity to see sites in preparation for restoration work and discuss the techniques to be used. She had plenty of time to take her planned stroll through the city and reach her destination to meet up with the group.

~

She arrived at the rendezvous to be welcomed by Anna and Stefano, whom she already knew, and who introduced her to their friends. She scanned the group and experienced a tinge of disappointment that Gio was absent. Soon Giulia joined them and hoisted a small pennant on a stick, raising smiles as she appointed herself tour guide for the day.

"Welcome to our visit today. We begin at this bronze equestrian monument, to Duke Cosimo I, commissioned by his son Lorenzino and executed in 1594 by Giambologna. The bronze reliefs around the base here represent Cosimo's defeat of the Sienese and his coronation by Pope Pius V in 1569. While you study the details, what can you tell me about Cosimo?"

Anna spoke first. "He rose to power in 1537 after his cousin Alessandro was assassinated. He came from a distinct branch of the Medici family and was appointed because Alessandro had only one illegitimate son, who was only four years old."

Giulia smiled her appreciation. "What do we know of Alessandro?"

Lucrezia felt bold enough to answer. "He was nicknamed 'the Moor' because of his dark colour; his mother was a servant of African descent. He was appointed leader of Florence in 1530 by Pope Clement VII, whom some people believed to be his father."

Giulia nodded, "Yes, Clement was the second Medici Pope, Giulio de Giuliano de Medici. The Medici had fled Florence in 1527 when the republic was reestablished. Alessandro's position was quickly strengthened when Emperor Charles V recognised him as Duke. Who knows how Alessandro died?"

"He was lured to a fake sexual liaison by his cousin, Lorenzino. I always check my dates out *very* carefully in advance," quipped Stefano, to general laughs from those assembled.

"Was Cosimo a dictator then?" asked another of the girls.

Giulia considered the question. "It's not really a term we apply to that period in history. He *did* sign an accord with the Council of Forty Eight, local nobles, but in reality it was an autocratic rule, firm but fair, rather than a democracy. Let's walk, shall we?"

She led them across the Piazza, passing by the reproduction of Michaelangelo's famous 'David' and pausing in front of the Loggia dei Lanzi and its collection of statuary. "Cosimo was an important patron of the arts. Inside Eleanora's apartments we'll see the work of Agnolo Bronzino, but who can tell me about the work which we're in front of now?"

Lucrezia recognised it at once. "It's 'Perseus with the head of Medusa' by Benvenuto Cellini," she offered.

Giulia nodded her approval. "Yes, awe inspiring, isn't it? It was created as a single cast, a fantastic technical feat, especially since no bronze statuary had been created in the preceding fifty years. Cosimo watched from the window of the Palazzo Vecchio as the statue was unveiled to a cheering crowd." Lucrezia looked up to the façade of the massive building, imagining the Duke waving to his adoring citizens.

They continued their walk towards the Arno, passing into the U-shape of the Uffizi. To their left, the usual huge crowds queued in noisy anticipation to gain entry to perhaps the world's most famous art gallery. As they walked, Lucrezia took note of the statues of the Renaissance giants watching over them. As they neared the river, Giulia stopped and raised her flag, bidding them to look up to the façade of the building. Lucrezia had been here several times before, but had never noticed the statue of a man in armour, standing imperiously above a river god and goddess and a shield bearing the emblem of the Medici, the *palle*.

"Cosimo began building the Uffizi in 1560, not as the gallery we know it for today, but as an administrative centre for the work of government. By now, he and Eleanor were living in the apartments in the Palazzo Vecchio that we're about to visit."

Stefano looked puzzled. "Why not make use of your own perfectly good palace?"

Giulia smiled; it was a good question. "Remember that Cosimo was leader of the Duchy now, effectively in sole charge. For much of the time, Florence had been a republic, ruled by an elected committee, the *Signoria*, and overseen by a *gonfaloniere*. Although the Medici were always powerful, they were not the only family of note in the city; each had their own *palazzo*, designed both for show and protection. The Palazzo here was at that time the seat of the government. Shall we go inside?"

The group followed Giulia through the entrance to the Palazzo Vecchio, happily bypassing the queue waiting for admission, and waited while she spoke to an attendant at the supervisor's office. Soon she emerged, brandishing a large key in triumph. She led the group up an impressive staircase and into a magnificent hall, the 'Sala dei Cinquecento'. Lucrezia gasped in awe at the sheer scale of the space.

"This is the largest space dedicated to government in the whole of Italy," said Giulia, pride in her voice. "Many times it was the seat of power of the Florentine republic, but Cosimo used it as a reception hall. Look in the centre of the ceiling - there Vasari painted the apotheosis of Cosimo." Lucrezia craned her neck to view the magnificent circular painting high above. She felt a tiny nudge on her elbow and looked to see Anna handing her a mirror. "Use this, it's easier." Smiling, Lucrezia realised that by holding the mirror low she could view the work, slightly magnified, in its surface. It was possible to make out Cosimo being crowned in laurel by a nymph, flanked by the cross of St. Stephen and the ducal crown. She imagined the sense of awe and intimidation which this space was intended to create in those seeking an audience with the Duke.

They passed through the hall and climbed a flight of stairs to a mezzanine, turning back on themselves and pausing on a balcony overlooking the great hall once more, to further appreciate its grandeur. Passing through a doorway they came to a barred gate on the right hand side, with a sign, 'chiuso al pubblico'.

"These are the chambers of Eleanora di Toledo," said Giulia, reverentially. "Restoration is about to start, we're so fortunate to be able to explore them on our own today!" She unlocked the gate and swung it open, flinching at the squeaking and grinding it caused. Once the group were inside, she closed and locked the gate and switched on the lighting.

"Cosimo and Eleanora moved here a year after they married, and Cosimo commissioned Bronzino and Vasari to carry out the decorative program. This is the 'camera verde', so called because of the green hue of the walls; sadly the original frescoes have been lost. The frescoes of the vault, by Ridolfo del Ghirlandaio have, however, survived."

Lucrezia, lingering at the back of the group, was only half listening. Her attention had been drawn to the small, jewel like chapel, with its magnificent frescoes. She recognised the work of Bronzino, whom she had studied extensively whilst in Oxford. To see this acknowledged masterpiece of Florentine Mannerism in such privacy was a consummate privilege for her. The frescoes of the walls depicted the story of Moses, while the vault depicted four Saints. On the back wall were three oil panels, an Annunciation flanking a Deposition. The whole had the effect of a jewel box, intimate and precious. Lucrezia imagined Eleanora reflecting in quiet prayer, completely at peace.

She felt Giulia's hand on her shoulder. "Majestic, no?" Lucretia merely nodded; words were not required. "The program to clean and stabilise the frescoes and touch up the surfaces of the panels will enhance its beauty even further. Who can suggests ways in which these works may have become damaged?"

Anna spoke first. "Frescoes suffer from moisture. These are internal walls, so ingress from outside is unlikely, but in cold weather condensation will form on the surface. That can cause growth of fungi and bacteria which can damage the surface."

Stefano added, "The calcium carbonate in the plaster can decompose, forming crystal salts which change or destroy the pigments."

"Very good," smiled Giulia, "what about the panels?"

Lucrezia suggested, "Humidity might cause the wood to warp, curving the surface and making paint flake from the surface. Smoke from the candles and yellowing of varnish will degrade the surface of the work, obscuring the colours below."

"Excellent," beamed Giulia. "Your next essay will be to formulate some solutions for these problems that restorers might utilise. Let's visit the other rooms here. The main feature in each is the ceiling paintings by Vasari, oil on wood panels."

Slowly they wended their way through the four remaining rooms, pausing to look at the ceilings with their gilded stucco and wood frames and central oil paintings. As they passed, Lucrezia tried to imagine Eleanora living here nearly five hundred years previously, spending most of that time pregnant with one of the eleven children that she had given Cosimo. He had remained faithful to her for all their lives together, extremely unusual for the times, and they had been fortunate to see eight of their eleven children grow to maturity. That point in her own life when she settled into marriage and a family life seemed impossibly distant. She had no particular inclination to settle down, envisioning a career first in her priorities, and her faith in marriage as an institution had now been severely dented by the traumatic separation of her parents. She had, deliberately, had little contact with them since arriving in Florence and felt a slight twinge of guilt about that. In particular, she worried about her father, who would be feeling very isolated right now. Her mother would be surrounded by sympathetic friends bemoaning the failures of the male of the species, and had the warmth of righteous indignation to fuel her.

She decided that she would contact her father soon, hoping to be able to bolster him somehow.

Eleanora di Toledo
Palazzo Vecchio
Florence, 1545

She kneels in silent prayer in the chapel, giving thanks for her children
and praying for safe delivery of this, her fifth child. She has been
blessed to survive four childbirths, to have all four children healthy and
for the continued love and devotion of her ever faithful husband. She
prays for Cosimo, once again gripped by quartan fever, shivering in his
quarters below, while the physicians bleed him and administer
belladonna. She welcomes the increased responsibility of government
he favours her with at these times, demonstrating his trust in her
administrative skills and popularity with the people. It has not always
been easy; many Florentines have been suspicious of a Spanish
duchess, but her willingness to learn their language, listen to their
representations and provide fair minded judgement when called upon
by their Duke to do so has softened their hearts to her.

She opens her eyes, welcoming the flickering candlelight illuminating
the jewel like interior of the chapel. *Signore* Bronzino has just finished
his fresco program, depicting scenes from the life of Moses. To her left,
he strikes the rock with his staff, bringing forth water, while his
followers gather manna. To her right, Moses and his followers cross the
Red Sea. Behind her, the miracle of the brazen serpent. She marvels at
the vibrant colours, the contorted twisted bodies and grimacing faces.
This is a new, stylised form of art, different from the geniuses of
Leonardo, Raphael and Michaleangelo. She smiles as she sees the
pregnant woman standing behind Moses as he strikes the rock; she is
now immortalised in this most holy of spaces.

Daily, she offers her devotions to the Deposition he has painted for the
altar, sharing in the suffering of her saviour and giving thanks for his
sacrifice. The Annunciation on either side reminds her of her blessing,
every year, of a new life to extend their burgeoning dynasty.
The whole decorative scheme has been carefully worked out between
her, Cosimo and the artist. It is both sympathetic to her own personal
piety and, with its meaningful relation to the Eucharist, in keeping with

the spiritual tradition of the Hapsburg dynasty, all the way back to its founder three hundred years ago, Rudolph I. It is typical of Cosimo to attend both to her personal wishes and the need to pay homage to Charles with such consummate ease; it is Charles, after all, who has restored the Medici to power and to whom continued gratitude is due.

She raises her eyes heavenward, drinking in the blue of the sky, framing the figures of the four saints, surrounding the depiction of the saviour. Saint Michael is sending Lucifer back to hell, Saint Jerome has his lion for company, blessed Francis and his brother are bathed in holy light, Saint John has both his eagle and his book.

Signore Bronzino is a genius, she thinks. His work with *Signore* Pontormo in the Capponi chapel provides a place I go to when I need solace and when we are at Poggio a Caiano, the beauty of his frescoes there surrounds me. Cosimo wants to decorate our villa and palace with magnificent tapestries and has asked Bronzino to draw the cartoons. His portraiture is consummate; how well he captured the spirit of Dante Alighieri and our friends at court, the Panciatichis. His depiction of Cosimo as Orpheus, painted before we met, hangs in the Medici Palace; I laugh when I see him looking so young and carefree. And naked too!

Yes, our lives are good, we are happy, our city is prospering and at peace. Maria, Francesco, Isabella and little Giovanni are thriving. When *Signore* Bronzino first painted me last year with Giovanni, I was so taken by his skills. He makes me look more attractive than I think I am, with the pride that I feel as a mother showing on my face. And that dress! It always was my favourite and you feel you could touch the fabric it looks so real. He read to me his poetry while he painted, his sonnets in tribute to Petrarch. He tells me that his art is an attempt to echo those ideals in pictures – radiant, compelling eyes, transforming gaze, alabaster throat, inner grace and virtue, pure hands of ivory. I blushed when he told me he aims to create a face so beautiful it outshines the sun! Perhaps he is painting me through the eyes of Petrarch contemplating his beloved Laura?

When he showed me his latest painting of Giovanni last month, I hugged him, I was so delighted! My little angel is laughing, so happy is my beautiful son. He *is* a good child but to see a portrait bring out the joy from inside him shows how talented our court artist is. And when visitors see his portrait of Cosimo in armour as they wait in the reception hall, they are reminded that, although a benevolent and caring leader, my husband will fight to protect what he believes to be rightfully his. And yet, we are fortunate to live in peaceful times.

She rises from prayer and walks through to the *camera verde*. Her lady in waiting, Donna Antonia, falls in silently beside her, opening the door to her dressing room, rewarded with a quiet smile. Donna Antonia guards access to her rooms, even when she is not in residence. She has some time to attend to some business matters so sits in her *scrittoio,* where she keeps all the records of her financial transactions. The production, acquisition and sale of grain has made her a very healthy profit this year. She looks up to the ceiling, where Salviati's frescoes have as their central figure *Dovizia,* the epitome of wealth and abundance, in celebration not only of her success in business but in tribute to her fecundity.

She hopes Cosimo might feel well enough to join her for supper this evening. He is just one floor below and soon she hopes she will hear his footsteps ascending the spiral staircase. A strong kick from inside her reminds her that soon another Medici will join the world.

Chapter 8
Florence
May 2018

It was Saturday, the day of the party at the Palazzo. Lucrezia had spent the day relaxing in the apartment, preparing herself for an evening of new faces and conversations, one which would take her out of her comfort zone. She had been made to feel most welcome by everyone, but felt a tad self conscious that everyone immediately defaulted to speaking English around her; she was determined to try to practice her unvarnished Italian on some of the more understanding students tonight.

She dressed in her finest frock, a plum taffeta dress cut off one shoulder and with an uneven hem. She felt comfortable in its modesty and yet a little bit glamorous. She had a set of pearl drop earrings and string of pearls which she had inherited from her beloved grandmother. Her shoes and jacket were beige and, for a bit of glamour, she took a gold clutch bag. She had never worn much make up, but applied a touch of blusher to her cheeks and, in an unusually brave gesture, a plum lipstick she had bought earlier in the day. As she checked her appearance in the mirror, she puffed out her cheeks and, with a whispered 'you've got this', headed out.

It was a balmy evening and she enjoyed the short walk along the *lungarno* to the Palazzo Moretti. Candles in wicker holders lit the entrance to the courtyard, which was similarly illuminated in the dusky evening light. Students milled around, holding flutes of champagne and chatting with members of the academic staff. Giulia spotted her at once and hastened over, looking stunning in a figure hugging black dress and gold jewellery. She kissed Lucretia on each cheek and steered her to a nearby waitress, who offered her a glass with a smile. "You look *bellisima*," crooned Giulia. "We'll mingle here for a few minutes then make our way up to the *terrazzo* where Tommaso Rialo, our patron, is going to speak. I'll see you up there." Waving across the courtyard, she sped off, leaving Lucrezia somewhat bemused.

She felt a touch on her shoulder and turned to see Gio, resplendent in dinner suit, grinning at her. "Hello again, Lucrezia, you look beautiful. Have you enjoyed your first week with us?"

She smiled, genuinely pleased to see him and once again struck by how handsome he was.

"Yes, thank you, everyone has been so helpful and the city is more beautiful than I could have ever imagined." She paused, considering her next comment, then decided to go ahead.

"I thought I might have seen you at the Palazzo Vecchio the other day." She'd been disappointed but sensed his ego could make do without this added stoking.

He shrugged casually. "My father is head of the restoration committee so I can go whenever I want to see it. I'll introduce you to him tonight."

The penny dropped. "So, you're Tommaso Rialo's son, right?"

He spread his arms wide. "Guilty as charged. But don't hold it against me, ok?"

She laughed, not quite knowing why, but suspecting that she was meant to. She sensed that, around Gio, there was an expectation that people would do what they were meant to do. She bristled somewhat at this recognition but decided not to be antagonistic. As she was pondering her response, Giulia began to ring on a glass with a spoon. "*Vieni di sopra per favore amici.*" Gio gestured for her to proceed him and she realised, somewhat to her annoyance, she was meant to accompany him.

On the terrace, a string quartet was playing Vivaldi and a warm zephyr stirred the air. Lucrezia felt the urge to escape Gio; she suddenly saw Anna and, seizing the opportunity, waved and made her way over. "*Ciao,* Lucrezia. You look very pretty," said her friend. Lucrezia smiled, relieved to be away from Gio, and started a conversation immediately.

Moments later, a deep voice requested silence and Lucrezia's attention was drawn to a small stage in the corner where a very tall, swarthy man stood, holding a microphone and gesturing for quiet. He was elegantly handsome with dark, wavy hair worn slicked back with oil, an olive complexion, hooked nose and dark eyes. He wore an expensive dark suit and white shirt, with a mauve silk tie and matching kerchief. In his hand, a cigar smouldered, producing a pungent smoke which wafted over the crowd. No one gave any sign of objecting. He exuded confidence verging on menace, even before he spoke. When he began, it was in a low growl, waving his cigar dismissively. Lucrezia simultaneously disliked him intensely and understood more about her reaction to Gio earlier.

He spoke quickly, in a strong accent, and therefore Lucrezia missed much of what he said. She understood something about a restoration project, about funding and about the honour this was bringing to the institute. Because she wasn't hanging on every word, she was able to watch and absorb the reactions of those around her. She sensed apprehension and wariness, as if they were in the presence of a dangerous animal who might attack at any moment. Who *was* this man and what hold did he exert over the institute?

As he finished speaking, he accepted the ripple of applause with a self-deprecating smile and a dismissive wave of his hand. He gestured imperiously to a waitress who rushed over with a brandy glass, filled with a generous measure. Lucrezia watched as Gio sidled up to his father, who embraced him and kissed him on both cheeks before putting an arm around his shoulder. They exchanged words before glancing over to Lucrezia, who realised she was the topic of conversation. Before she could escape, Tommaso waved to her to come over; the onus was on her and refusal was not an option. Lucrezia had always intensely disliked being told what to do, often opting for the polar opposite course of action in defiance, but she knew that that was not a wise choice in this moment. Fixing a smile on her face, she flicked a quick gesture of her hand to Anna, imploring her to accompany her, but the slightest shake of the head and Lucrezia was flying solo. With growing apprehension, she strolled as casually as she could across the terrace.

Tommaso was positively leering by the time she reached him. He extended his hand and, when she went to shake, bent to kiss it instead. She resisted an urge to wipe her hand on her dress and instead offered, "*Piacere di conoscerti.*" He smiled ingratiatingly and gave a slight bow. "The pleasure is all mine, young lady. My son has told me of the English rose who has brightened up his class. He does not exaggerate when describing your beauty."

If there were a chauvinism contest between Gio and his father, both were scoring A plus. "You're too kind," she offered, keen to move the conversation on. "I'm afraid my Italian is substandard and I missed some of your speech."

"I'm happy to fill you in. I was explaining how, in my role as advisor to the Opificio delle Pietre Dure, I have been able to secure the contract for restoring the chambers of Eleanora for the Institute of Fine Art restoration here at the Palazzo. You may be thinking that, as a patron of the Palazzo that constitutes a conflict of interest, but I assure you I have no financial links with the Institute and my decision has been ratified at board level in the Opificio and by the Friends of Florence, who will be funding the work."

"I saw the apartments the other day, they are so beautiful. It's heartening to know that work is being undertaken to preserve and restore them."

"Yes, we'll be using the latest technology too. I would be happy to show you more once the work is underway."

'*As long as there are lots of people around,*' thought Lucrezia, smiling as if this would be the treat of a lifetime.

"Please excuse me now. I'll leave you with my son." At that, he headed towards a group of women and left Lucrezia back in the clutches of Gio, who was aiming one of his fawning smiles at her. "He's not so bad, really," Gio said; was her expression *that* obvious? "He gets things done, makes things happen. It's important in a world where there's often too much talk and not enough action."

"Oh, I don't know, I enjoy a good conversation and action's sometimes overrated," said Lucrezia, fighting a losing battle to disagree with everything Gio said. He didn't take the bait, simply nodding enigmatically. "Can I get you a drink?" he offered.

"Please, just a white wine." As Gio headed for the bar, Lucrezia searched frantically for an escape and jumped at the opportunity to engage Laura and Sofia in conversation. When Gio returned with her drink, she took it with a smile, immediately returning to the discussion with her girl friends. Gio stood for a moment, scowled and slunk away. Seeing Lucrezia relax, Sofia smiled. "Not blown away by our resident Casanova I see?"

Lucrezia laughed and wrinkled her nose. "That obvious? There's just something about him I don't like…"

"Oh, he's not all bad," said Laura. "At least you're know where you stand with him."

"He doesn't want you *standing* at all," protested Sofia. "Now, kneeling or lying down, *then* you've got his interest!"

All three girls burst out laughing, attracting the attention of those around them, and drawing daggers from Gio, which made them laugh all the more. Lucrezia was feeling the wine going to her head, surprisingly so, for she hadn't had that much, she thought. Perhaps it was because she hadn't eaten. She decided she would head home early and cook herself some pasta. She bid a fond goodnight to the girls and headed downstairs.

Down in the courtyard, she stopped by the office to say goodnight to Giulia, who was working on a document. She offered to find someone to walk Lucrezia home, but she declined with a nonchalant wave of the hand – it was only a few hundred metres along a busy road. She pulled on her jacket and slipped out of the doorway. She did not notice that, as the door was closing, a dark shadow slipped out behind her.

~

Next morning, the sun was already up and the apartment was flooded with daylight. Lucrezia had a pounding headache and felt nauseous. She had fallen asleep immediately on coming home, without making anything to eat. She couldn't believe how hung over she felt after so little alcohol, but she couldn't really remember that much of the evening; perhaps she had drunk more than she thought? She poured herself a large glass of orange juice and searched for some paracetamol. As she put the coffee maker on, she was surprised by a pounding at the door.

Opening it, she was confronted by two police officers, a man and a woman. They flashed badges but she didn't really have time to register. "Lucrezia Sims?" asked the female officer.

"Yes, my god, what's happened? Is it my dad?"

"You need to come with us to the station," said the officer, making no attempt to explain why.

"I don't understand. What's wrong?"

"We need to ask you some questions."

"I'm going nowhere until you explain what is going on?" Having no experience of dealing with the police, Lucrezia was scared.

"Very well. You have been accused of assault and we need to question you under caution."

"That's ridiculous! I haven't assaulted anyone! If you won't tell me then I'm saying nothing and going nowhere."

The officers exchanged glances and the male nodded. The female stepped forward. "Lucrezia Sims, I'm arresting you on suspicion of assaulting Gio Rialo. You can have a solicitor appointed and should say nothing that could incriminate you until then."

Shock. Incredulity. Absolute confusion. Numb, she allowed herself to be led away, placed in the back of the police car and driven through the streets of Florence.

~

As soon as they arrived at the station, Lucrezia realised she needed to use the bathroom. Her request was granted, but she was accompanied into the lavatory by a female officer and told to leave the cubicle door unlocked. Her mind racing as to what she should do next, Lucrezia became aware of a discomfort when she passed urine. That was unusual for her, but she had bigger problems to deal with. As she wiped herself, she noticed blood on the toilet paper; strange, her period wasn't due. Gingerly she explored herself and felt a stinging pain when she touched her labia. A sickening thought dawned on her. Feeling strange at the party. Patchy recollection of the evening. A disproportionate hangover. And now this. Had she been drugged and assaulted?

She stumbled out into the corridor again and called to the officer. "I think I've been drugged and sexually assaulted." The officer shook her head. "That's not how this works; you're the one accused of a crime here."

She was led into an interview room, where the female officer who had arrested her was seated beside a short, obese, jowly man, who looked deeply misanthropic. His collar was unbuttoned with his tie haphazardly tucked under it. His hairline was receding, his deep set, shifty eyes glanced up at her and he sighed, waving her to sit.
"I'm detective Esposito. This interview is being recorded."

"Wait, I think I've been drugged and assaulted..."

By way of response, Esposito let out an even louder sigh and dealt out a set of black and white photos, with the air of a croupier at a poker table. "Gio Rialo doesn't look his normal handsome self today."

The photos showed Gio, face on and in profile, his left eye bruised to the point of closure, his nose swollen and deviated, his lower lip split and his right earlobe torn. "Add in three broken ribs and a possible ruptured spleen. You're stronger than you look, young lady."

"Wait, you don't think *I* ...it's not possible."

"He swears you did it. Witnesses have you leaving the party together. He says you went crazy, accusing his father of touching you up at a party and then grabbing a tree branch on the pavement and hitting him repeatedly."

Lucrezia laughed. "That's *insane!* I left the party and went home because I felt strange. I can't remember anything after that until I woke up."

Esposito shrugged. "How convenient."

"I think he drugged me and assaulted me. I've been injured in my private parts. I demand to see a doctor."

Esposito threw his hands up. The female officer leaned over and whispered in his ear, which seemed to exasperate him still further. "Sure whatever. Why stop at one crime when we can have two to investigate?" Shaking his head, he stormed out.

The female officer smiled sympathetically. "We'll send for a doctor. Can I get you a drink?"

Lucrezia was weeping now. She managed to ask for some water then sat with her head in her hands, disbelieving of what was happening. She strived to recall anything from the night before but it was a complete blank. Could she have done these things under the influence of alcohol?

It was completely out of character. And if she *had* assaulted someone, how could she have just headed off home and gone to sleep in her own bed? Gio had brought her a drink, it would have been easy for him to slip something into it, then follow her home and force his way in as she opened up the apartment. And then….Oh God, not that…

~

Half an hour later, the officer returned and ushered Lucrezia to an examination room, clinical and cold, where a stern faced doctor sat behind a desk. Not bothering to introduce herself, she commanded Lucrezia to strip, place her clothes in the evidence bag and dress in the gown provided.

"But these aren't the clothes I was wearing last night," she protested.

"Just do it. Please."

Soon Lucrezia was dressed in a thin paper gown and lying on a cold couch. "Open your legs. Wider." The doctor touched her, causing her to flinch with pain. Without warning, she parted Lucrezia's labia and inserted a swab inside. Then she turned and pulled the screen around.

"Can I get dressed?"

"No. We'll bring you scrubs soon. I need a blood sample."

The doctor returned, applied a tourniquet and, without swabbing the skin, roughly inserted a needle and then a vacutainer to draw a sample of blood.

"What's that for?"

"Toxicology."

"What did my exam show?"

"Some slight scratches. Have you had thrush or anything that would make you itch?"

"Wait – you seriously think I did that to myself? I demand to see someone else."

The doctor drew back the curtains with a snap and glared at Lucrezia. "You will. Detective Esposito. Goodbye."

She left, slamming the door. Moments later, the female officer returned with orange scrubs akin to prison attire and told Lucrezia to get dressed.

~

Back in the interview room, Esposito reiterated the accusation that she had repeatedly struck Gio Rialo with a length of wood, rendering him unconscious. He had been found by a passer by and taken to hospital where he had quickly regained consciousness. His injuries were not life threatening. He had given his sworn statement to police. A witness had given a statement that he had seen a couple, the female fitting her description, arguing outside the Palazzo Moretti at the time Gio reported being attacked. She would be brought before a prosecutor within twenty four hours and should seek to engage a solicitor. She could make a phone call to do so.

"What about my claim that I've been drugged and assaulted?" she asked, desperately.

"The officer here will take your statement," answered Esposito, more kindly now. "May I suggest you make your call first?"

~

Having no one to turn to, Lucrezia asked for the number of the Palazzo Moretti. Thankfully, Giulia was at work and answered on the first ring. She listened dumbfounded as Lucretia unfolded her story and immediately offered to send a friend who was a lawyer to represent her.

"Please, will you phone my father, let him know what's happened?" she sobbed.

"*Tesoro,* of course. Don't worry I'll get you through this."

After her call, she sat with the officer giving her statement. But what was there to tell? She'd been at the party, she'd spoken with Gio, yes, she felt strange so left early. There were huge unremembered lacunae. Her story, indeed her whole world, was falling apart.

Chapter 9
Florence
May 2018

Lucrezia sat in Giulia's kitchen, nursing a glass of wine, staring out of the window. For now, she was at liberty, the prosecutor having determined that there were insufficient grounds to prosecute at present, asking instead that the police carry out further enquiries. Meantime, Lucrezia had been discharged to the care of a responsible person, surrendered her passport and agreed to report to the police station on a daily basis. She was immensely grateful to Giulia, who had provided a solicitor for the hearing and, not only readily agreed to act as guarantor, but insisted that Lucrezia move out of her apartment and in with her. Her husband, Antonio, was an art dealer and was currently in the Far East negotiating sales, so there was plenty of space.

Lucrezia had endured a tortuous, emotional phone call with her father, who was planning his trip to Florence to support her. After his initial shock, he had been incandescent with rage at her suspected attacker and at the police for their insensitive handling of the matter. He had deflected her attempts to discuss his own troubles and whether he had made contact with her mother; none of that mattered, he said.

Giulia bustled over and deposited a plate of *spaghetti al vongole* in front of her. "*Mangiare,*" she urged, gently. Lucrezia smiled and pushed the food around the bowl with her fork.
"We should go out this afternoon," suggested Giulia, breezily. "I have to pop in to the restoration centre where the girls are working on 'The Last Supper'. I'd love to show you how we do it."

Lucrezia smiled, feeling a deep affection for this caring woman and realising that she dearly would love to be outside and focusing on something other than her own woes. "Thank you, I'd like that."

On impulse, she asked a question which had been on her mind for some time. "Giulia, do you have any children?"

Giulia looked wistful. "No, my dear, I'm afraid not. I had a very complicated miscarriage some years ago which left it impossible for me to conceive again. It is the one single regret I have in an otherwise wonderful life."

"I'm so sorry."

"But why? It happened long ago and I rarely dwell on it. I have my students to remind me of the joys of youth and many, many interests and friends to focus my energies upon. Now, shall we go?"

~

It was a fine, warm afternoon and the centre of Florence was heaving with visitors. Lucrezia and Giulia strolled past the front of the Duomo and paused to admire the spectacular doors of the baptistery facing the façade, Ghiberti's famous 'Gates of Paradise'. Lucrezia had spent an hour in front of the original doors in the Museo del'Opera del Duomo, marvelling at the naturalistic details of this seminal work of the Renaissance. She was delighted to have been able to do so, as the throngs of people milling around the metal barriers outside made obtaining a decent view of these replicas nigh on impossible. She marvelled at the beauty of the figures, particularly Joseph, who stood with his right heel raised in the depiction of his uncertainty. The bronze head of the creator of these magnificent portals gazed out in pride from between the panels. Lucretia pondered how the beauty of the art on display in Florence contrasted with the hidden depravity into which she had been sucked.

They continued around the baptistery, turning onto Via de Martelli, and soon the mighty Palazzo Medici-Riccardi arose imposing on their left. "Just imagine all that went on within those walls," said Giulia. Lucrezia nodded; the Medici had ruled Florence, or been major players in its republican government, for millennia. Studying their family dynasty had been the most rewarding way in which she had formed a synergy between her two greatest passions, art and history. She felt a twinge of sadness as she recalled passionate discussions with her mother, who from a historical perspective had viewed the Medici as a despotic bunch, in opposition to Lucrezia's more favourable depiction of them as patrons of the arts. She hoped her mother was coping; she had deliberately not contacted her, deciding that she would leave it to her father to decide how, if at all, to involve his wife in what had transpired.

By now they had walked along Via Cavour and reached Piazza San Marco. From the far corner of the square came the excited hubbub of the crowds thronging to the Galleria dell'Accademia to pay homage to Michaelangelo's giant 'David'; Lucrezia was glad that they took the opposite quieter turn and, within moments, stood outside the restoration workshops of Advancing Women Artists. She followed Giulia inside and stood in awe at an immense canvas, supported on wooden struts, around which half a dozen women worked in companionable silence.

Several raised a hand or voice in greeting, and Giulia called out a cheery salutation, so quickly and somewhat lost in the cavernous hall that Lucrezia did not catch her meaning.
"Come, I'll show you what we're doing," she beamed, taking Lucrezia by the hand as if she were an excited child. She led Lucrezia around behind the huge canvas, where a woman sat perched on a stool, peering through a large magnifying glass at an area illuminated by a spotlight. "Maria, this is Lucrezia," said Giulia. The woman leaned back, smiled and stretched, clearly relishing the break from her painstaking work. "Can you show us what you're doing?"

"*Ovviamente,*" smiled Maria, rising and gesturing for Lucrezia to take her seat. "In this area, there are two small holes in the canvas. Because they are so small, we try to match the actual ends of the individual fibres and glue each separately. See?"

Lucrezia peered through the magnifier, marvelling at the skill and patience required to execute such painstaking labour.

"But here," Maria continued, "the hole is larger, so we have had to use a patch, which we applied and then heated with a small iron. Not only does this cause the patch to adhere; the lining compound penetrates through into the original canvas and holds down loosening flakes of paint."

Giulia smiled her thanks, and led Lucrezia around to the front of the massive canvas. "Stand back to take in all its magnificence before we look closely," she suggested. Lucrezia walked to the entrance of the hall and turned to face the painting. It was, as befitted the subject, a wide canvas, depicting Christ, tenderly embracing John, flanked by his disciples, one at each end of the table framing the scene, and Judas depicted in front of the table. In contrast to other depictions of the famous subject, most notably that of Leonardo da Vinci in Milan, rather than the background being open, this scene was set in front of a continuous wooden screen. This rather detracted from the views of the human figures, in Lucrezia's opinion, but the presence of a bright white tablecloth somewhat mitigated this. The main colour palette was of greens and oranges. From a distance it wasn't easy to read the faces of the disciples but the position of their bodies imparted a sense of anxiety to the developing situation.

Giulia waved her closer, inviting her to join another restorer working on an area at the right hand side of the massive canvas. "Arianna, this is Lucrezia. Can you show her some of the techniques we use here?"

"Sì.. Ciao, Lucrezia. Here I am simply cleaning the surface of the canvas with water and solution of olive oil soap; it's very gentle but surprisingly effective at removing the grime." She moved a foot or so to her left, indicating an adjacent, brighter area. "Here, with the grime removed, you can see the varnished surface. Notice how the varnish has changed with age, yellowing and thickening to be opaque – we call that 'bloom'. Here we are gently removing the varnish with solvents; when we have repaired any areas of paint damage, we will apply a conservation grade varnish that will remain clear and bright."

Lucrezia nodded. "How do you make sure the repainting remains faithful to, and blends in with, the existing painting?"

Arianna smiled; it was a pertinent question. "First we have to attend to the existing paint. Where possible, we would readhere any flaking paint, to retain as much as the original surface as possible. We use a dilute gelatine solution which we dry with a micro hot air tool. For small flakes we use a magnifier or even a microscope." She moved towards the centre of the work, where a colleague sat with palette and brush, applying paint to the surface of the work. "As you can see, sadly, large areas of this canvas were badly damaged when it was removed from its frame and stored rolled up." She shook her head at the desecration visited on what was clearly a beloved work. "Carlotta is using pigments which we have adapted in the workshop, to ensure that not only do they match the existing oils but they do not change colour with time. Also, it's important that our retouching can be removed at any time during future restoration. In the past, using oils which altered their hue with time and which were ineradicable caused more damage that that already present in the work."

"How fascinating. Thank you for giving me an insight in to the wonderful work you do. It must be intensely gratifying."

Arianna smiled. "It most certainly is. You would be very welcome to come back, we could show you how to contribute your own mark on the *rinascita* of Plautilla's masterpiece."

Lucrezia was touched by this show of kindness, at a time when her faith in humanity had been badly shaken. "I'd like that. I will come back. *Grazie mille.*"

Leaving the restorers to their work, Giulia and Lucrezia headed outside. Spotting a restaurant with views of the church and convent of San Marco, they agreed to stop for lunch.

~

Feeling restored herself by the first decent meal she had been able to eat since her ordeal, Lucrezia nursed her glass of wine and decided to press Giulia about what she had witnessed at the party.

"I couldn't help notice that Tommaso had, shall I say, an *unsettling* effect on people the other night? It was more fear than respect I felt. I hope I'm not speaking out of turn?"

Giulia took a long, slow sip of her wine before replying. "No, after what happened to you, you deserve some answers. I've been crucifying myself for not speaking much sooner. Tommaso is….not to be trusted. Perhaps even dangerous. There are many rumours about him, many. From shady business dealings to involvement in organised crime. Ours is a small, peaceful city, his presence is, for many, a blight, a stain on the beauty we take such pride in. He is patron of our institute and responsible for the work that comes our way, which both provides opportunities for teaching and the income that sustains our organisation. No one dare take issue with his…methods. As the person with whom he deals at the Palazzo, he affords me a modicum of respect and I take a path of least resistance in return. He is not a man to antagonise."

Lucrezia pondered her next remark, but she trusted Giulia and for the first time felt ready to talk about her nightmare. "I was getting a similar feeling around Gio. A menace, a sense that he owned and controlled you, that you were to do his bidding or else…"

Giulia reached over the table. "I will always blame myself for letting you leave that party alone. I share your opinion of Gio; how do you say in English – 'the apple doesn't fall far from the tree?' I should have warned you…."

"No, no, it's not your fault. It's not *anyone's* fault but Gio's. I'm convinced he drugged and assaulted me, but the police don't seem interested and there's little chance he'll even be charged." Lucrezia stared despondently into her glass.

"Even the police are reluctant to move against Tommaso, I'm afraid. Some people hint that the police themselves are complicit in his corruption but I myself think that Esposito is simply navigating the easiest route to his retirement. I'm sure when your father arrives he will have a meeting with him to try to press them to act."

Lucrezia's father was arriving that afternoon, having caught the first available flight. He had said little in the few brief conversations they had managed, focusing on the practicalities, like his flight times and where he would stay. Lucrezia and Giulia were meeting him at four o'clock at his hotel, near Santa Maria Novella. He had given no indication whether he had spoken with her mother but the fact that Lucrezia hadn't received a call suggested that her mother might still be blissfully unaware of all that her daughter had been through. In some ways, Lucrezia hoped this was the case, reluctant to add even more pain to an already harrowing time. She wondered if her family's misery would ever abate.

Chapter 10
Florence
May 2018

They sat in sullen silence in the bar of the hotel. Jeffrey looked exhausted and, Lucrezia thought, had clearly lost weight. After a tearful reunion, and his expression of his profound gratitude to Giulia for taking care of his daughter, he had retreated into his shell, contributing little to the conversation. Lucrezia fought down a rising tide of anger at his ineffectual unwillingness to take charge of the situation. She was also angry that he had refused to inform her mother, which seemed more about staying out of the firing line than sparing Marie any distress. She loved her father, always had, but he was presenting as cowardly and feeble when she required his protection.

Giulia, sensing the impasse between the two, attempted to inject some momentum to proceedings. "Are you going to request a meeting with the police, Jeffrey? I could have my friend, who represented Lucrezia, accompany you if you are?"

Jeffrey stopped swirling his brandy in its glass and looked up, quietly nodding. "Yes, yes, I think that would be helpful. But I have no idea how to go about arranging an appointment."

"I could have Simona do it for you. Shall I call her?"

Jeffrey nodded and Giulia took her phone from her bag and stepped out into the foyer. Lucrezia took the chance to press her father. "Dad, you're *miles* away. What's eating you?"

Jeffrey shook his head sadly. "The first requirement of any father is to protect his child and I've failed you, twice now. I know what a shock it was for you to discover what I'd done all those years ago. I understood why you wanted to come here, to get away from all the sadness at home but look what's come of that now."

Lucrezia barely recognised this weak, self indulgent man as her father. "Dad, we all make mistakes. And what happened to me here has absolutely *nothing* to do with how good a father you are. You're here, aren't you, to support me and to help me get justice? Let's focus on that – how to make things better now, rather than dwelling on the past."

He seemed comforted by that, even managing a weak smile. "Thank you. You know how proud I've always been of you. How proud we *both* are." He defocused as he receded once more into a quagmire of guilt. Lucrezia threw him a line.

"I think you're right to protect mum from this. It will be better if I call her when we've resolved matters with the police. There's nothing she can do right now and she would want you here, protecting me."

At that, Giulia returned and sat down. "Simona has arranged for you to meet with Detective Esposito tomorrow at ten am. She will meet you in the foyer here at ten minutes to ten and accompany you to the interview. She suggested you remain with me, Lucrezia, and I concur. I'm going to leave you both to enjoy a quiet dinner together. Shall I come back and meet you here, Lucrezia, shall we say ten pm?"

They agreed on this plan, and Giulia left, embracing Lucrezia and shaking hands formally with Jeffrey.

~

The following morning, Jeffrey and Simona sat in the interview room at police headquarters, awaiting Esposito. 'This is nerve wracking, and I've done nothing wrong,' thought Jeffrey. 'I can only imagine how Lucrezia felt, sitting here accused of a crime she didn't commit while believing she herself was the victim. This must be his way of intimidating us, Esposito, keeping us waiting like this.'

As if cognisant of this allegation, the door opened and Esposito shuffled into the room. Jeffrey's initial impression was of a man thoroughly defeated by the world he was forced to inhabit. A man living in one of the most beautiful cities on earth who viewed its charms from the gutter, surrounded by the dregs of humanity. Esposito extended a chubby, sweaty hand, mumbled an introduction and sat heavily down at the table. Rather than initiating conversation, he merely folded his hands on his corpulent abdomen and flicked his gaze between the two people seated opposite, as if puzzled by their presence.

Simona took the initiative. "Thank you for seeing us. As I'm sure you appreciate, Mr. Sims has some questions about his daughter's experiences and how they were handled by the department."

Esposito nodded. *"Bene, certamente.* Exactly how can I help you sir?"

Jeffrey spoke slowly, suppressing his anger. "I'm wondering why my daughter was arrested and charged when she, herself, was the victim here."

Esposito nodded, slowly, thoughtfully. "If I may, there are two questions here. Firstly, your daughter was arrested as there was evidence, both from the victim and an eye witness. It is our law here, you may not be aware, that all those arrested are brought before a prosecutor within twenty four hours; in this case, the decision then taken was to release your daughter, while we carried out further enquiries. I am happy now to inform you that, having done so, we are dropping all charges against your daughter."

Jeffrey sat back, puffing out his cheeks in relief. "Thank you, that is good news. But, what about her accusations that she was drugged and assaulted?"

Esposito was nodding, anticipating this line of questioning. "She provided us with a statement, but her memory of the evening was very hazy – she had been drinking, no? There are no witnesses as to anything untoward having taken place."

"Have you questioned this boy, this Gio Rialo?"

Esposito reclined, his arms spread wide. "On what grounds? Because she *thinks* he might have followed her and attacked her? We have no basis on which to interview him."

Jeffrey glanced over to Simona, who nodded; clearly, she agreed.

"But what about the medical examination? She told me she had clear signs of injury to her private parts."

Esposito referred to a sheet of paper in front of him, turning it over, before nodding and replying. "The doctor found only minor marks, such as one might inflict upon oneself if scratching an itch. Not consistent with non-consensual sex."

Jeffrey raised his voice, resisting the urge to rise from his seat. "That's ridiculous! She was in considerable discomfort and tells me she still has pain and swelling."

Esposito held up the paper with a shrug. "The medical evidence is quite unambiguous, sir."

"What about the toxicology? Lucretia drank very little that evening, certainly not enough to impair her memory. We're certain that that boy put drugs in her drink, probably Rohypnol."

Esposito raised both hands. "Be very careful *signore,* that is a serious accusation and we have laws of slander to consider."

"Well, what were the results, man?"

Esposito searched through the papers several times, a puzzled look on his face. He pressed an intercom on the desk and rattled out a stream of Italian, way beyond Jeffrey's comprehension.
He turned to Simona for help. "The result isn't in the file; he's having someone check for it."

Esposito sat back, quietly waiting. Suddenly, he leaned forward, looking more animated than at any point during the interview. "A suggestion, sir, a 'word to the wise' I believe you say in English. I would be very careful about bandying round allegations regarding the Rialo family. *Signore* Tommaso is one of our most noteworthy citizens, also a man with a reputation for, shall we say, *resenting* unwanted or unfair publicity. He would make a very poor choice of enemy. I counsel caution."

Jeffrey was, by now, considerably riled. "Are you saying he's above the law? Untouchable? Or are you scared of him? That's it, isn't it; like police everywhere, you're looking for the easy targets, not the real criminals."

Esposito remained calm. "I refute those suggestions sir. I was merely trying to provide you with some friendly advice. We have no reason to take any action against any member of the Rialo family."

At that, the intercom buzzed; again, Jeffrey did not understand the message being conveyed.
Esposito spoke quietly. "I'm sorry sir, the laboratory have no record of ever receiving the sample. It was logged out for this office but never arrived for analysis."

Jeffrey started out of his seat; Simona reached out a restraining arm, shaking her head. Stunned, he sat down. Simona spoke for him. "Thank you for your time this morning, detective. We'll show ourselves out."

~

Back at the hotel, everyone was speaking at once, trying to make sense of the morning's revelations. The news that she no longer faced charges had been an immense relief to Lucrezia, who had wept in her father's arms. But the apparent cover up of medical evidence, which rendered her accusations against Gio baseless, stirred emotions in the group. Simona seemed to regard the proceedings as standard practice and Giulia was similarly sanguine.

"It stinks of a cover up, surely?" fumed Jeffrey. "You're always hearing how corrupt the Italian police are!"

Giulia and Simona shifted uncomfortably in their seats. "I'm sorry," said Lucrezia, "we're just upset."

Giulia smiled at her. "That's entirely natural, we understand. The relationship between Tommaso Rialo and the law has always been, how shall I say, fluid. And although I entirely believe you regarding what happened, Lucrezia, I have to admit I cannot see a way to implicate Gio in the proceedings, no matter how disagreeable we all find him."

Lucrezia knew she was right, but Jeffrey was having none of it; he was scenting blood. "Perhaps I should have a chat with this Gio - no one has asked his take on it. Does he have an alibi?"

They all spoke at once. "He doesn't need one…", "That would be a very bad idea…", "No *way,* dad…" Tempers were running high, emotions threatening to render reason obsolete.
It was Giulia who poured oil on troubled waters. "Let's all just take a deep breath and let things settle. I need to check in at the Palazzo, Simona, I know you have clients this afternoon, Jeffrey you haven't seen anything of our beautiful city. Why don't you let Lucrezia show you around, then I'll meet with you both this evening to decide where we go from here? *Concordato?"*

Lucrezia seized the chance to calm her father down. "That's a wonderful idea. Come on dad, there's so much beauty on view simply walking around. Let's stroll through the centre, stop for a glass of wine, pretend we're tourists just for a couple of hours? How about it?"

Jeffrey sighed, then nodded in agreement, taking his daughter's hand in his. "I'd like that."

~

The Duomo complex, with its cathedral, baptistery and *campanile* was familiar to Jeffrey from pictures, but the scale surpassed his expectations. Lucrezia worked hard to engage his interest, picking out some of the less obvious sights – the statues portraying the Baptism of Christ by Andrea Sansovino, above the Gates of Paradise, the hexagonal panels on the lower level of Giotto's *campanile,* by Andrea Pisano, depicting scenes from Genesis. Together they walked down Via dei Calzaiouli, window shopping in the stores, stopping outside the church of Orsanmichele.

"It's like a who's-who of sculpture," said Lucrezia, excitedly. "These arches were originally open when the building was a grain market, but were filled in in the fourteenth century to form a church used as the chapel of all the important guilds. Each one commissioned a statue of their patron saint to stand in their niche. There are works by Donatello, Nanni di Banco, Verrochio, Brunelleschi, Ghiberti and Giambologna. My favourite is this one, 'Christ and St Thomas', by Verrochio. Look at the folds of the garments and the natural way St Thomas's foot comes right out of the niche!"

Jeffrey smiled, enjoying seeing his beloved daughter reinvigorated by the healing power of art. Not for the first time, he wondered at the inherent duality of man; the ability to create such beauty and yet the power to inflict such cruelty on others. He took Lucrezia's hand and smiled, as they strolled in the afternoon sunshine.

Chapter 11
Florence
May 2018

Jeffrey had decided he was ready to head back home, feeling much
more reassured now that the charges against Lucrezia had been
dropped. The episode of her amnesia and the suspicion around it still
niggled away, but he recognised that there were, indeed, no grounds for
the police to proceed. Giulia had given her reassurance that she would
look after Lucrezia, who could continue to live with her for a further
week until her husband returned from his travels in the Far East, and
Lucrezia had regained much of her enthusiasm for the fantastic
opportunity that this gap year represented.

Jeffrey remained at the hotel that morning, organising his afternoon
flight and dealing with some issues which had arisen at the university
back home, while Guilia offered to take Lucrezia to view some art.
"Are you feeling energetic today?" asked Guilia. "There's much I'd like
to show you."

Lucrezia nodded enthusiastically; a day looking at art was precisely
what she needed.

"*Bene.* I've based the day around two artists I know you're keen on –
Plautilla Nelli and Andrea del Sarto. We'll be rather off the tourist track
too, which is nice. Do you fancy a stroll along the banks of the Arno?"

Together, they turned their backs to the Ponte Vecchio and strolled
along with the Arno on their right. After thirty minutes they turned left
into the narrow streets behind Santa Croce and soon stood outside the
refectory of San Salvi. Giulia opened the door and they entered: no one
else was there. On the far wall was depicted a magnificent 'Last
Supper', resplendent in iridescent hues of purple, orange, turquoise and
green. Lucrezia drank it in, feeling the healing power of the beauty of
art. Guilia spoke quietly beside her. "*Guarda,* the way Jesus's fingers
entwine with John's, *delicatamente.* And the small balcony above with

two observers. Andrea del Sarto was at the height of his powers when he worked here in 1526 and 1527."

Lucrezia had seen this work online when she was studying the Mannerist period, but no illustration came close to conveying the chromatic splendour of the work.

Giulia called her over to two small panel paintings displayed on the opposite wall. By contrast with the fresco, these were dark, brooding works; in each, a figure in a light garment was portrayed against austere, gloomy landscapes. Lucrezia looked puzzled; "I don't recognise these."

Giulia pointed first to the work on the left. "'Saint Catherine Receives the Stigmata' and 'Saint Dominic Receives the Rosary', both by Plautilla Nelli. We restored these both in the Advancing Women Artists workshops in 2008 and were struck by the solemnity of the pieces. But we must remember that this was the time of the counter reformation and the Council of Trent, when art had to follow strict guidance and be devoid of personal feelings. And she was still living in a Dominican convent at the time, where the influence of Savonarola persisted long after his death."

Lucrezia looked from one end of the room to the other, at two styles of art some half a century apart, expressing diametrically opposed philosophies and yet each, in its own way, magnificent.

They exited into warm sunshine and strolled through empty residential streets, passing the *campanile* of Santa Croce on their left. As they approached the Hospital of Santa Maria Nuova, a cacophony of sirens reminded them that this was a living, breathing city, not merely a museum; even here, life and death crises were part of the everyday tableau. Soon they were once more in Piazza San Marco, with Giulia asking Lucrezia to wait outside the convent while she spoke to an attendant. Minutes later, they both beckoned Lucrezia in through a side door, which led into the museum. "I know you're all coming to visit the convent and see the marvellous works of Fra Angelico, but Nelli's

'Lamentation with Saints' is here in the museum; my friend kindly let us in free." Lucrezia smiled her thanks to the attendant.

"Plautilla was, as you know, a nun in the convent of Santa Catarina di Cafaggio, which stood near here. This work, we restored in 2006. What do you think of it?"

Lucrezia studied the piece, keen to practice her ability to systematically analyse a work. She took in the city walls in the background, the three crosses high on the left and the holy family huddled around the dead Christ in mourning. "The colour palette is much brighter, especially the blues and oranges, but the figures are strangely static and emotionless. I guess it's as you explained earlier, art conforming to the religious dictates of the time."

Giulia nodded. "That's good. We should never overlook the aesthetic qualities of a work of art, but understanding the context in which it was created can enhance our understanding and enjoyment. Are you too tired now or can you take some more?"

"More, please!" said Lucrezia, enthusiastically.

Giulia laughed, pleased to see her friend happy, and beckoned to her to follow. A few hundred metres took them to a small door marked 'Chiostro dello Scalzo'. "The portico to this church was designed by Guiliano da Sangallo, who much later redesigned St Peter's basilica in Rome. Inside is a series of monochrome frescoes which del Sarto worked on between 1509 and 1526. They depict the life of St John the Baptist plus four virtues – Faith, Hope, Charity, Justice. I'm going to order us a drink at the café there while you go inside. *Vino bianco*?"

Lucrezia nodded gratefully and entered the cloister. It was shaded, cool and empty. Around the walls of the small space was a series of wonderful frescoes, which clearly showed the artist's change in style from late Renaissance to full Mannerism, the figures harmonious, complex, full of movement. It was wonderful to see the development of a movement within a single space and she strolled around the whole quadrangle, in splendid isolation, several times, before joining Giulia across the street.

They sat enjoying the crisp, cold wine, indulging in the favourite Italian pastime of people watching. Lucrezia marvelled at the style and elegance so effortlessly displayed and mentioned it to Giulia. She smiled. "We call it *sprezzatura,* the art of looking good without trying too hard. It's an old concept, from a book I'm sure you'll know, Baldassare Castiglione's 'Book of the Courtier'." She paused for a moment. "It's sad your experience has been as it has; most Italian men are actually very polite and respectful of women. Please do not take the Rialo's as archetypal."

Lucrezia was ready to move on. "I know. I'm sure the other students will convince me of that. I'm not looking for love at the moment anyway; after what happened with my parents I'm favouring extending my single lifestyle for the foreseeable future."

Giulia gave a strange, nostalgic smile. "I was born and raised in Sicily. There, *sprezzatura* is a requirement for every man! I've never seen so many mirrors and so many men looking in them. It was a very masculine culture sadly and I don't believe it has made a great deal of progress since then. My father was a very powerful man; Tommaso reminds me of him sometimes. I remember people saying they were scared of him, when I was a little girl. We were a very wealthy family and I have my suspicions about how that wealth may have accrued." She sighed, perhaps realising she had said too much. "*Comunque,* we lived in a very beautiful part of the island, the Val di Noto, near Syracuse. There are some beautiful baroque buildings in the towns in the region."

"Do you ever return there?"

"No, my parents both died many years ago and I have no family left on the island. It belongs to another life. I inherited a considerable amount of money when they died so I am fortunate that I can dedicate my life to my love of art. It is as a champion of art and its restoration that I would choose to be remembered."

"You seem very happy here in Florence."

Giulia smiled reflectively. "I've been lucky with my husband. We were childhood sweethearts and then met up again at University. As far as I can be certain, he still holds only me in his heart. If I'm honest, the thing I fear most in life is the march of time. I'm ridiculously vain and not proud of the fact that I've resorted to cosmetic procedures to preserve my looks. Please keep that as our little secret!"

Lucrezia wondered how much wine Giulia had drunk before she rejoined her; her tongue was considerably looser than usual. She opted to play along, responding with a conspiratorial wink. "One would never know. You're a very beautiful woman."

Giulia raised her glass with a smile. "Antonio tells me the same and I choose to believe him.
His work keeps us apart too often, but some space in a relationship can be healthy I think. Certainly there's no risk of over familiarity. My work at the institute and with AWA keeps me busy here and I'm comfortable with my own company. Florence is a welcoming community; those of us who live here are intensely proud of our heritage and it's surprising how well we handle all the things a big city needs without ripping the heart out of it."

"Well, I've been made most welcome. It's a shame my dad had to visit under the circumstances he did, but I'm here for another year and hopefully he'll come back when we're both in better places. Speaking of him, we'd better think about heading back."

Giulia checked her watch. "One more quick stop? Santissima Annunziata is just around the corner; the atrium has wonderful Mannerist frescoes and inside the church is the most important Marian shrine in Florence. We can make it easily."

The church was indeed but a few minutes distant. Immediately inside the façade, before the entrance to the church itself, was a large, enclosed atrium. The walls were covered with bright frescoes.

"Thankfully, the frescoes had been detached, renovated and replaced in the 1960s, which saved them from much of the damage of the 1966 flood. Friends of Florence cleaned and repaired them between 2013 and 2017. This area was completely open air until 1833 and the roof covering wasn't put in place until a hundred years ago. I'm going in to pray at the Chapel of the Most Holy Annunciate, immediately on your left as you enter. Join me when you've seen the frescoes. And don't forget to look at the bust of del Sarto!"

Lucrezia ambled across to read the descriptions of the works. In this space, the *Chiostrino del Voti*, Andrea del Sarto had first frescoed scenes from the life of Saint Philip Benizzi of the Servite order. Then he was asked to return to paint two further works, 'The Arrival of the Magi' in 1513 and 'The Birth of the Virgin' one year later. The presence nearby of Pontormo's 'Visitation' and Rosso Fiorentino's 'Birth of the Virgin' made this a haven for admirers of Mannerist art like Lucrezia. Conscious of her time, she made a mental note to return here at her leisure and entered the gloomy church interior.

On her left stood an intricate *tempietto,* within which was an altarpiece. People were lighting candles, standing with heads bowed or, as was Giulia, kneeling in prayer. The atmosphere was reverential. Wanting to avoid disturbing the peaceful atmosphere, Lucrezia instead took out the pocket guidebook she always carried. Just able to read in the gloom, she learned that one Fra Bartolommeo had fallen asleep while painting the panel, struggling to complete the face of the Virgin. When he woke, the piece had been completed by angelic hands. Word of the miracle spread, establishing the church as a Marian shrine and a place of pilgrimage. Although not religious, Lucrezia could respect the power of faith that had pervaded the Middle Ages.

Giulia appeared by her side, looking serene, and together they walked the short distance through the streets to Jeffrey's hotel. Giulia took a seat in the bar, while Lucrezia went to check if her father was ready to depart. She found him all packed, reading a novel and looking much more relaxed. He embraced her at the door.

"Thank you so much for coming, dad. Please check in with mum as soon as you get home, let her know what happened now that everything's fine. And take better care of yourself, for goodness sake!"

Jeffrey smiled as he reached for his suitcase. "Yes, darling, I shall. It's my job to worry about you, though, not the other way around."

They continued the amiable banter until the lift deposited them in the foyer. Giulia came to meet them and offered to call Jeffrey a cab, an offer which he gratefully accepted. As she made the call, he was confused to see Esposito, flanked by two uniformed officers, enter the foyer; they spotted him and approached.

"I hope you're not leaving, Mr. Sim," said Esposito, voice dripping with sarcasm.

"Actually, my plane leaves in three hours. What do you want?"

"Gio Rialo was found beaten up this morning. One hour ago he died of his injuries. I need you to come with me for questioning under caution, charged with his murder."

Chapter 12
Florence
May 2018

Jeffrey stood stunned, Lucrezia cried out, Giulia ran to comfort her. "This is ridiculous, I've been nowhere *near* that boy.." began Jeffrey.

Esposito raised a hand. "I would advise you to appoint and consult a solicitor before you speak, *signore.*"

"He's right," added Giulia. "I'll have Simona meet you at the station."

"Thank you. Lucrezia, could you call Andrew Pennington and set up a call with him? I'd like his take on things."

Lucrezia just stood, open mouthed. This could not be happening…

"I'll do it," offered Giulia. "His number?" She wrote in on the back of her hand as Jeffrey rattled it off. "Don't worry, you know Lucrezia is safe with me. We'll work through this."

Esposito was extracting a set of handcuffs from his pocket. "Surely that's not necessary," cried Lucrezia.

"It's fine, darling, go with Giulia please," said Jeffrey, softly, extending his arms.

~

Lucrezia sat sobbing on the bed as Giulia called Andrew Pennington from her balcony. She took in the view of her beautiful city, stung by the emergence once again of its dark underside. She laid out the scenario to Pennington and set up a time for him to speak directly with Jeffrey.

"It sounds like your friend is more than capable of representing Jeffrey through the court process," said Pennington. "I know a chap in Fiesole,

Marco di Luca, who used to be in the security services – he left in 2007 when they were restructured. Now he's a freelance private investigator. He's well connected in the Florence scene, both above and below the law, a kind of cultivated Philip Marlowe. Shall I give you his number?"

Giulia agreed and then checked with Lucrezia. "I think we need someone to do some digging as to exactly what's going on here," she agreed. "This whole thing's been peculiar from the moment I got arrested and the authorities are either incompetent, suspect or both. Can we meet this *Signore* di Luca please?"

"*Va bene.* I'll call him now."

Moments later, Giulia came in from the balcony, nodding. "He'll meet us. We can go now; he wants us to go up to Fiesole to see him. I feel like escaping the city for a few hours anyway, don't you? We'll get the bus from Piazza San Marco."

~

An hour later, the ATAF bus pulled into the Piazza Mino, disgorging the passengers who had made the thirty minute climb from Florence below. It was a beautiful spot, cooler than the oppressive city, with spectacular views to the Arno valley below and the majesty of the jewel of the Renaissance. Across the square stood the cathedral and adjacent to that the café where Marco had arranged to meet them. They strolled over and a tall, dark man rose, waving in greeting. As they introduced themselves, Lucrezia took in his square jaw with its days growth of stubble, piercing blue eyes and and nose which looked like it had taken its fair share of blows. He wore a dark tee shirt and chinos and had a large military looking tattoo on his right biceps. He bristled with physical and emotional energy. She immediately felt safe in his presence.

"Thank you for agreeing to meet with us," she began. "I believe Giulia has outlined all the terrible things that have happened to us. Do you think you can help?"

Marco took a drink from his beer and nodded slowly. "All I offer is to scratch around, to see if I can pick up any threads. You might be surprised how much nefarious activity goes on in Florence - it's a microcosm of Italy and, sadly, our country has a poor record on corruption, even at the highest levels. I was with the security services for many years but quit in 2007 when they were restructured after yet another scandal and the AISI, Agenzia Informazioni e Sicurezza Interna, was formed. I'm still in touch with some of their operatives and even some officers inside the police. But I guess I'll find out more from my contacts in the darker corners of the city."

Lucrezia could have hugged him. "Thank you *so much*. I wish I'd never met the Rialo's, they've been nothing but bad luck."

Marco scoffed contemptuously. "They are very bad news, *signora*. I have long suspected them of being involved in highly dangerous and illegal activity, but whenever I've asked around, I've had doors slammed in my face. Tommaso Rialo is a very clever, very treacherous man."

Lucrezia looked crestfallen – surely her father was yet another victim of this man's heartless drive to achieve his nefarious ends? Marco noticed her sadness and spoke up. "Gio's death, however, clearly means something has gone seriously wrong with whatever Tommaso is developing. This is just the moment to act; people will be talking. I will begin immediately while the 'iron is hot', as you English like to say."

Lucrezia looked uncomfortable. "We're not rich people, I'm not sure how…"

Marco waved a hand dismissively. "I was fully intending to root around anyway, see what they're saying on both sides of the law now that this has come to pass. Give me twenty four hours and meet me here again. If I think I can help you, then we can talk terms. Ok?"

Giulia smiled to see the relief on Lucrezia's face. *"Grazie mille,* Marco. We shall be here the same time tomorrow."

~

Lucrezia's heart was lighter on the return trip to the city. At last there was some hope of untangling the complex puzzle in which she and her father were ensnared. She turned to Giulia, but found her gazing pensively out of the window, deep in thought.

"Are you alright?" she asked her friend, solicitously touching her shoulder.

Giulia started. "Yes, of course, sorry, I'm just a little tired, so much has happened. Let's go straight back to my flat and call Simona, shall we?"

~

An hour later, Giulia finished her call and smiled at Lucretia. "They haven't charged your father, they haven't enough evidence for that. But because of the seriousness of the charge they're detaining him for forty eight hours to carry out further enquiries. Simona knows little more than that. Your father is in good spirits and has spoken to his lawyer in Oxford, so he knows about Marco. She'll call me tomorrow after we've met him again and before she visits your father. You should try to rest now; I need to go to the Palazzo for an hour but I'll be back and I'll cook us some dinner."

She took her jacket and, rather abruptly, left the flat.

~

Giulia did not go to the Palazzo, instead she headed to the Piazza della Signoria and stood on the corner, her conversation masked by the noise of the tourists. Her call was answered on the second ring, by a deep voice. *'Pronto?'*

"What the hell is happening? How did Gio die?"

'Thank you for your sympathies. It was meant to be a warning. He was getting too close, sniffing around where he shouldn't be. My associate was somewhat overeager. He has been appropriately chastised.'

"God, you're a cold hearted bastard. He was your *son*! And what the hell were you thinking assaulting that poor girl. Can't you learn to keep it in your pants?"

'The thrill of the chase, you know me. Keep calm, there's no evidence linking me to her. If Esposito knows what's good for him, he'll get Gio's death pinned on her father. I have a few handy witnesses lined up primed with what to say.'

"She's hired a private investigator, an ex-security operative, Marco di Luca. He's started sniffing around."

There was a derisive snort down the phone. *'That clown's been after me for years. He's a washed up has been, he's got nothing and never will have.'*

"Don't be so sure. You're getting careless."

The growl was deeper now. *'And you are forgetting to whom you're speaking. More respect in future. And remember, I own you – one word from me and you're finished."*

The line was cut, leaving Giulia staring at her phone, oblivious to all the beauty surrounding her.

Chapter 13
Florence
May 2018

The following lunchtime saw Lucrezia and Giulia back up in Fiesole to meet Marco, who was awaiting them at the very same table when they alighted from the bus. After exchanging greetings, Lucrezia asked if he had been able to make any progress.

He nodded. "It is interesting, there is clearly something afoot. A well known thug from the *oltrarno* was found floating in the river this morning. A friend of his, who has acted as informant for me previously, believes he was killed on Tommaso's orders, something to do with Gio's death. One rumour is that this person failed in his duty to protect Gio, another that he was somehow involved in Gio's death. There's also a buzz around increased incidences of people being paid to deposit multiple small amounts of cash in bank accounts linked to Tommaso. It's been rumoured for as long as I can remember that he's involved in money laundering but we've not been able to prove it. This pattern of activity is often the initial part of that process."

"How does that link to my father?" asked Lucrezia, anxiously.

Marco shrugged. "I'm not sure. But everyone is aware he's being made the 'fall guy' for Gio's murder. The question is why Tommaso should be trying to cover up his son's death instead of taking his revenge; that's much more his style. Word is, I'm afraid, that several people have been bribed or threatened into giving false witness statements implicating your father. Many people are either too poor or too scared to resist Tommaso."

Lucrezia's heart sank; they were powerless in the face of such power and corruption. Marco sensed her despondency and tried to lift her spirits.

"All is not lost. We can fight fire with fire. I have a friend, a woman who has good reason to despise Tommaso Rialo. If I ask her she would be prepared to give an alibi for your father, say that they spent the night together. It would at the very least secure his release from prison."

Lucrezia hesitated; she despised the idea and suspected that her father would, even more so. Was this the level to which their lives had descended?

"Not everyone is in thrall to the Rialo's; he's stepped on many toes and there are those who would dearly love to see him brought to justice. I have a colleague in the intelligence services who's attempting to examine Tommaso's financial dealings and an interesting lead among the artisans on the *oltrarno* who are getting fed up of being threatened. I've got hold of a few threads; let me pull away and see what unravels."

Lucrezia breathed a sigh of relief. "Can we talk about your fees, please?"

Marco looked uncomfortable, as if caught in the horns of a dilemma. "There is one approach which may provide a way of gaining some leverage, but which would require you to do something I suspect would distress you. I am in two minds as to even suggest it, but I think it might spring us an opening."

Lucrezia pressed him. "Tell me. Anything."

He studied the table top closely. "I believe something very bad happened to you last week, something for which Gio was blamed?"

Lucrezia's heart raced; she felt dizzy and nauseous. "Go on…"

"My plan would require you to go back to the police and report the incident again. This time with a witness."

Lucrezia looked puzzled. "But Gio is dead, what is the point in that?"

"It was not Gio that my witness saw, *signora.*"

"Then who? For god's sake just tell me!"

"It was Tommaso."

Lucrezia sat stunned, disbelieving. Memories of the shock of her arrest flooded back to her, but still there were huge lacunae in her recall of the events of that night. Not him, oh no, not that…She burst into tears. Giulia hugged her tight, glaring at Marco.

"I'm sorry, but I believe it is information you deserve to know. My source is prepared to give evidence if he is offered protection; to be honest, he has several reasons to want to make himself anonymous. More difficult will be getting Esposito to act on the evidence; he's clearly beholden to Tommaso is some way. But even laying the accusation will occupy Tommaso so much that I'll have time to root around while he's looking the other way. Perhaps he might even trip himself up. It's a great deal to ask though…"

Lucrezia was composed now. "It's the right thing to do. Not the easy thing, but sometimes that's the way of the world. For me and for my father."

Marco nodded. "Many others would benefit from seeing Tommaso brought to justice. It would give me great pleasure to be part of his downfall. That is all the reward I would seek from you."

Lucrezia understood the bargain she was striking. She could no longer sit back and accept the deceit visited upon her. The cost of justice for her and her father was to be the humiliation of a public rape trial. If that was what it took…She reached across and shook Marco's hand. "Whatever it takes to stop these people."

~

"They're coming after you; he has a witness to last Saturday. How could you have been so careless?"

'Witnesses can easily be bought or scared. If she goes to Esposito he will deflect suspicion from me. You worry too much..'

"Marco di Luca *does* worry me; he knows what he's doing and he's coming for you."

'Let him. Things are moving well and all the necessary steps are being taken. No one will connect the pieces. You'll have your share soon – maybe use it to get some therapy for your neuroses.'

~

The next morning, Simona and Lucrezia waited outside the police station; Marco was meeting up with his source and bringing him, under safeguard, to give his statement implicating Tommaso in Lucrezia's attack. Simona checked her watch nervously; they were late. "Perhaps he's having second thoughts," Lucrezia said, anxiously.

At that, Marco appeared, practically dragging a weasel-faced man who looked anxiously around him. He was unkempt, sweating and smelled strongly of alcohol. If this was their best hope…

Marco practically threw him up the steps to the station, nodding for Simona to take him inside. As they did, a car pulled away from the corner opposite the police offices, its lights dimmed.

Chapter 14
Florence
May 2018

Jeffrey shuffled into the visiting room and sat heavily down opposite the glass screen. Lucrezia leaned towards him, touching the glass, tears streaming down her face. She picked up the phone, but her father simply stared past her as if she wasn't there. He looked haggard, with bags under his eyes, and even though it had only been two days since she had seen him, he looked even more emaciated. Prison life was clearly destroying him.

Finally, he jerked upright and picked up the phone, attempting a smile but failing miserably. "Hi, darling, how are you?"

"Oh daddy, this is terrible. Simona says they can hold you another seventy two hours without charge after the prosecutor hearing today? What did he say?"

"Well, I didn't understand a word but apparently they have two witnesses who saw me confront Gio in the street and push him. And I have no witnesses to my being in my room alone all evening. So Simona says I'm in serious trouble; she thinks they'll charge me."

Lucrezia knew she had to do it. "Marco has a friend, a woman. She's willing to testify that she met you in the bar and spent the whole night with you. It'll give you an alibi."

Jeffrey actually laughed out loud. "Are you *serious*? What would your mother say?"

"Jesus CHRIST dad, don't you get it? This is *murder,* you could spend the next twenty years of your life in an Italian prison. Mum's sensitivities are the least of our concerns right now!"

Jeffrey was riled now, shouting his fury at the screen. "Right, I know, Tomasso Rialo is coming to get me. Simona says he's even more angry now that you have a witness against him! Some help *that* was!"

Lucretia was puzzled. "What *exactly* did she say?"

"She overheard him on his phone outside the police station as she came out. He was coming out from giving his statement about Gio's death. He said something about us having a witness against him, something that happened last weekend."

Lucretia's heart leapt into her mouth. "I need to make a call."

~

Outside, she dialled Marco's number; he answered immediately and asked what was wrong; she should only call in an emergency.

"I think we have one. Did you tell anyone, *anyone,* about the witness who saw Tommaso following me the night I was attacked?"

"Of course not, it's vital we protect him; his life would be in danger if Tommaso got wind of it."

"Precisely. And yet he knows; my father's solicitor heard him talking about it. How could he *possibly* know?"

And then, with complete clarity and chilling certainty she knew exactly what had happened.

~

Back in the prison visiting room, Lucrezia outlined her new suspicions to her father, who listened with mounting incredulity. "Who *are* these people? How can they be so despicable, so evil?" His head dropped into his hands, the picture of utter despair.

Lucrezia started to cry. The one person in Florence who had taken her to her bosom, been her friend and mentor, had betrayed her. Her father, who was now implicated himself, had lost the will to protect her. She felt utterly alone.

She put her hand on the glass screen, reaching out to the man who had built his world around her, now infinitely distant. Jeffrey raised his head; Lucrezia shrank back, not recognising the face confronting her. His eyes burned with hatred, his teeth drew back in a snarl, the tendons in his neck stood out in restrained fury. "I'll do it," he hissed. "Enough. I'll take her alibi, I'll get out of here and we'll fight them. No more being pushed around. I'm your father and those who come for you will find me waiting."

Eleanora di Toledo
Palazzo Vecchio
Florence, 1545

Cosimo and Eleanora sat together in companionable silence having finished their supper. As the servants cleared away, Eleanora raised the issue that had been on her mind. "With our fifth child soon to be born, God willing, I have been thinking much about how we can best prepare our children for their future lives."

Cosimo smiled benevolently; he liked it when his wife felt comfortable enough to address him directly with her concerns. "I too have found the matter on my mind. Since my mother died two years ago, I am aware that more of the responsibility passes to you and we are blessed to add another child with each year that passes! And we take responsibility for Bia and Giulia, in addition to our own. Our children are our future."

She smiled secretly. Cosimo made so secret of the fact that he aspired to see his children as future rulers, clergymen and consorts. She played directly into his line of thinking. "The education and fashioning of our children plays a critical role in the lasting political efficacy of our dynasty. Our children could be mobilised as future consorts, courtiers, military leaders, high ranking clergy, even monarchs."

Cosimo visibly swelled with pride. "As I see it, we have two sets of priorities: to position our children for potential strategic international alliances and, at the same time, to maintain our regional power base by demonstrating continued loyalty to our Florentine traditions."

Eleanora nodded; she recognised that perhaps their greatest triumph as rulers had been achieving exactly that bridge – successful international players, strongly allied to the Holy Roman Emperor, yet intimately connected and sensitive to the needs of the Florentine people.
By marrying Eleanora, Cosimo had produced children with aristocratic blood who had a legitimate claim to a place among European nobles, but the Medici had to hold to their Florentine identity or risk the goodwill of their subjects. "We are a unique and powerful union,

husband and our children require an education bridging the needs of both royal children and those of wealthy merchants. The models in use today perhaps poorly serve to provide what we require."

Cosimo agreed. "Children of wealthy merchants are often educated at home or in small schools while children of princes are sent to other courts or condottieri. For children of merchants, education involves study, recreation and adopting the social, professional and political responsibilities of their families, whilst sons of princes are sent to Spanish and Papal courts to develop specialised skills – graceful speech, hunting, jousting, preparation for a cardinalate. There is a dichotomy there, an inherent schism which does not, I think, best serve our needs."

Eleanora came to sit beside her husband and took his hand. "Your wisdom and attention to my needs never dwindles, my darling. We have achieved much together. Together we can plan a system which will prepare our children in ways which will distinguish our dynasty and secure Medicean ambition." She spoke wisely, using that latter phrase as a stick with which to prod Cosimo's desire.

"We come from such different backgrounds and yet, united, we are an unparalleled force. I was raised in Naples from the age of ten and educated according to practices of the Spanish court, while you, husband, continue to respect the traditional venerable practices of your famed ancestors. Each of our ways has much to offer. Do you share my vision of a future where we combine the best from each of our cultures and engage with current philosophies circulating both in the Florentine court and internationally, to produce an education for our children which stands above anything anywhere in Europe?"

Cosimo found his wife inspiring at moments like these. He always admired her vision and single-mindedness, tempered by her wisdom and her unfailing ability to always afford him his rightful place as head of the dynasty. "Tell me, where do you think we should begin, my duchess?"

She sat upright; clearly she had something prepared. "The humanists tell us that education should begin in infancy; toys such as dolls, swords and hobby horses should be chosen to direct children towards their future roles by age four or five. We have done that too, haven't we – a doll for Maria, an alphabet toy for Francesco. They divide growth stages into seven year periods: birth to seven is *infanzia*, seven to fourteen *puerzia.* At seven, they dictate that boys and girls should diverge; a formal education for boys, domestic training and religious education from their mothers for girls. Matteo Palmieri defines fourteen as the age of reason. Girls are divided into pre- and post-menstruation, which only signals their eligibility for marriage."

Cosimo laughed, bewildered by the tornado of information. "And your point, good lady…?"

"My *point* is that this allows other people to decide who and what our children are, what and when they should learn, and, therefore, who and what they can *become.* I desire our children to be the very best they can be, the very best of *each of us.* That, husband ,would be a towering achievement and secure our dynasty and our legacy!"

He embraced her warmly, thrilled by her passion; she was physically trembling with excitement. "So, do we completely start afresh or can we make us of existing teaching?
I think we need to try to reconcile the humanist programmes, which you know impress me, with the morality-based teachings of the church. The Council of Trent has passed new guidance reminding us of our Catholic virtues. There are two main curricula, our traditional Italian *'studia humanitatis'* and, as I am well aware you know, the Jesuit *'ratio studiorum'.*

Eleanor gulped, aware of Cosimo's resistance to the Jesuits, whose cause she had tried, thus far ineffectively, to advance in his eyes. Thankfully he did not stumble over this hurdle; indeed, when he continued it was with both magnanimity and humility. "I have always allowed, and indeed encouraged you, to adhere to the customs of your homeland. My adoption of Spanish customs demonstrates my fealty to you, my love, to the imperial family and to our Toledan relatives. Passing on Spanish traditions will also enable the children to participate in diplomatic exchanges as they will be familiar with etiquette, dress and language."

He dropped to one knee before her and took her hand. "I have a vision, a dream, one where we create a model incorporating the very best elements of Florentine humanist, bourgeois, princely and Spanish pedagogy. Each of us can exert their own influence derived from the traditions of the class and culture of our own upbringing. A model which incorporates the practices of merchant and noble classes, social and intellectual traditions long established and new courtly standards introduced by the best contemporary leading humanists. Together, we will provide our children with the best education anywhere in the world!"

She laughed with joy, thrilled to see the man she loved so enthused. "Our curriculum will cover everything the children of merchants and nobles could need! Instructions in religious and social graces. Knowledge of the religious authors, the ancients such as Cicero, Livy, Virgil, moral philosophy, history and poetry, as well as scripture and philosophy. Grammar, mathematics, religious and civic duties. Instruction in the liberal arts, in dancing, hunting, fencing, horsemanship, fine manners and music. Our children shall be proficient both in Latin and Greek with a separate tutor in each, and our daughters shall also learn Spanish, making them eligible for advantageous marriages."

Cosimo laughed. "Wherever shall we find the time?! It shall be the duty of both of us parents to oversee their education. I shall enlist a team of tutors, renowned intellectuals and promising young scholars alike, to whom we shall provide an education themselves. We shall attend lessons with our children and direct what texts they should study. As I am often absent, will you maintain communication with the tutors to monitor the children's progress?"

"Of course, husband. Do you think our children should share the same tutors and be offered the same curriculum early on? Their later education could become more specialised depending on their gender and the role we see ahead for them?"

Cosimo thought carefully. The children conformed in public to strict gender roles and he was keen for that to continue. Despite favouring equality and high standards for *all* his children, he could clearly see that their final polish would be dictated by whether they were intended as a consort, a military leader or a cardinal.

"I think that exposure to the same curriculum for the princes should be extended to the princesses, which I know is unusual. Then they should also receive education in courtly matters to help us secure marriages for them. The princesses could also be trained in music, dancing and horseback riding. It is my opinion, however, that they should be less visible in public, helping to promote their eligibility as consorts by maintaining the prized female virtues. As Vives says: 'A good woman will stay at home and be unknown to others, retiring and silent, with eyes cast down, so that some may see her but none will hear her.'"

Despite being a strong advocate of a woman's rights, Eleanora accepted that her husband had a valid point. Their discussion was more focussed around what a woman *could* achieve than what was denied to her. She took her courage in her hands and raised a potentially thorny issue. "Can I return to our traditional Italian *'studia humanitatis'* versus the Jesuit *'ratio studiorum'*?" She sensed Cosimo stiffen, but pressed on. "I would like to ask Diego Laínez to develop an educational model following the Spanish and Catholic models of my family. Something which approximates to both curricula? I know you have reservations about the Jesuits, but it's important to me and you can trust me to check every detail with you for approval."

Cosimo choked down a sense of irritation; they had made huge progress in their discussions and he wasn't going to let the annoying Jesuits get in the way. He simply smiled in agreement. Indeed, he offered a final olive branch.

"You introduced an internationalism to our Florentine court when you arrived in all your beauty – your costume, manners and language. I would like our children to reflect that as they grow. You may choose how they dress for state occasions. In addition, I have asked *Signore* Bronzino to make his services available to you whenever you request them, to commission a portrait of yourself or any of the children, to make a permanent record of our family."

Deeply touched by this token of affection, Eleanora took her husband in a warm and long embrace.

Chapter 15
Florence
May 2018

"It *must* have been her; there's no other possible explanation," said Lucrezia, swallowing her rage as she tried to assimilate the extent of her betrayal. "They must be working together."

The morning paper had carried the headline story of yet another suspicious death in the city the previous evening. A small time petty criminal had been found with his throat cut in a backstreet of the *oltrarno*. Rumour had it that it was related to turf wars over drug dealing; Marco knew that Tommaso had acted with lightning speed and ruthless efficiency to silence the witness against him.

Marco nodded. They sat inside the cathedral in Fiesole, speaking in hushed tones, watching the entrance. "I'm afraid you are correct. I never imagined her capable of such things; she is held in very high esteem in the art world. I cannot imagine the depth of her entanglement in Rialo's affairs. And yet, this presents us with an opportunity…"

"I don't understand."

"Whatever either of us say to her will be fed directly to Tommaso. He will react without questioning her; clearly he trusts her already and her providing this covert information to assist him will only enhance that trust. So, essentially we can manipulate him by feeding him information. That way, we could lure him into taking action that might show his hand."

Lucrezia considered this; it was a bold plan. Could it work? "What exactly are you proposing?"

"Can you get access to Giulia's phone?"

"I think so, yes, for a moment. She often leaves it on the table while she's in the bathroom or the shower. But I don't know how to unlock it."

"That doesn't matter. You'll only need access to the device for thirty seconds or so."

~

That evening, Giulia cooked dinner for Lucrezia. They spoke about her father and the result of his appearance before the magistrate. Giulia shared some small talk about the Palazzo. Taking her courage in both hands, Lucrezia began. "Marco called me today. He thinks we should go around to my apartment and search it for evidence, you know, from the night Tommaso was there. He's got a forensic kit; he could dust for fingerprints, check the bed for hairs and so on. I said I'd meet him there tomorrow."

Giulia paused for a moment. "*Bene,* I'll come with you."

"No, it's ok thank you. I have to get used to being back there sooner or later. I'll meet up with you after you're finished at the Palazzo."

Giulia smiled thinly. "I need to pop over there now for an hour, I'll just change into something warmer." She went through to her bedroom, leaving her phone on the kitchen work surface. Quickly, calmly, Lucretia slipped a small device from her pocket and inserted it into the charging port on the phone. A red light began to flash rapidly on the device. "Come on, come *on..*"
The red light stopped, Lucrezia pulled the device from the phone and took a bottle of wine from the fridge as Giulia returned.

"One for the road?" she asked brightly.

"Perhaps when I return," answered Giulia as she left.

~

Outside she dialled Tommaso's number. As his phone began to ring, Marco activated the flashing icon on his laptop and hit 'record'.

Eleanora di Toledo
Palazzo Vecchio
Florence, 1547

She read the letter again, folded it carefully then put it away in the desk
in her *scrittoio.* and came through to kneel in the *capella.* She felt that
her spirituality was changing, away from the traditional devotional
habits she had inherited from her mother in a treatise that she herself
had commissioned as a young woman when she married Eleanora's
father at the tender age of thirteen. For years now, she had practiced a
spiritual exercise for half an hour before sleeping, contemplating her
sins and the thousand sufferings they caused Christ and his blessed
mother.
The Jesuits were offering a new way.

Last year she had met one Father Juan de Polanco, recommended to her
by Ignatius of Loyola. Polanco had come to prominence whilst
preaching in Pistoia, reaching the attention of Cosimo, to whom he had
been presented in Pisa. He had written to Eleanora, stating that the
Jesuits were capable of assisting the duchy by means of prayers,
admonition and advocating on their behalf in the sight of the Divine
Mercy. He listed her enemies, including excessive involvement in the
education of her sons, superfluous expenditures, haughtiness and
idleness. There was a time that she would have bristled with the
suggestion that anyone dare advise her on how she handled her
children, but she was older now, more secure in her position and
prepared to take such well intentioned advice. Polanco had also
suggested that she should take a confessor, someone who would also
give her instructions for the spiritual life.

Unfortunately, Cosimo remained deeply suspicious of the Jesuit
movement; he mistrusted their involvement with the still present
Savonarolan movement in the city and the *piagnoni,* the 'snivellers',
who continued to hold republican sentiments. Because of this, he had
refused to countenance founding of a Jesuit school in any of the cities
of the duchy and Eleanora, wisely, had not pushed the point. He had
agreed, however, to her having spiritual advice in private from Polanco,

who was now a frequent visitor to her apartments. He had attended strictly on the sufferance of Donã Maria de Contreras, the formidable companion in charge of her principal chambers and a woman who devoted her life to the safety and happiness of the duchess.

Cosimo was not an unreasonable man and he was prepared to tolerate a Jesuit presence in Florence. Father Diego Laínez was now preaching in the city and was the one visiting her in her apartments to provide spiritual guidance. Whenever he and his colleagues visited, she liked it that they behaved in accordance with the Spanish manner, kneeling before her and asking for her hand in greeting, hats off. Her uncle, Don Pedro, a frequent presence in her household, was the promoter of the Jesuits in the city and she liked dealing with Spanish members of the Jesuit order. They needed her help to counter a diffidence towards them by Florentines and, in addition, she constantly played intermediary between the Jesuits and Cosimo.

As she became more self assured and grew into her role as duchess, she felt a growing confidence. She knew she was more than Cosimo's wife and the mother to his children and, to be fair to him, he recognised that and afforded her active roles in governing, as well as a complete free hand in her business affairs. Her desire to see the Jesuits establish a teaching college in Florence was another chance to test her mettle.

Chapter 16
Florence
May 2018

It was time to make the next move in flushing Tommaso out into the open. Marco had been thinking about his friend's comment that there were rumours of multiple small deposits into accounts under Tommaso's control. He recognised this was often the first step in a complex money laundering process and one that, because of the small amounts of each transaction, was difficult to monitor. He would need to provoke a much larger transaction if the authorities were to detect it.

He had an ex colleague, Taddeo, who now worked for the Giuardia di Finanza and was part of the team who monitored electronic transfers, trying to pick up any unusual activity for further scrutiny. Marco called him and outlined his suspicions.

"*Si.* It is currently impossible to screen for multiple small deposits; we have neither the technology nor the manpower and, besides, this is the mainstay of multiple small businesses who have cash takings and bank them at regular intervals. We focus on transfers in excess of €200,000 normally, but, of course, it depends on the destination of the transfer too. Any deposits into offshore accounts or to the Far East attract our suspicion that someone may be layering."

Marco recognised this as being the second stage in the money laundering process. "Why the Far East?"

"There's been a rapid escalation in the number of underground banking systems and alternative banking platforms there, particularly in China. They've developed bespoke online software which encrypts and manages transactions, without the regular audited due diligence checks. Is your suspect dealing in commodities? If not, he might be dealing in cryptocurrency and that's nigh on impossible to detect I'm afraid."

"We're still building a case, but yes, we think there are commodities involved. I'm hoping I can prod him into acting hastily; if I give you a heads up, can you move immediately to surveillance?"

"Of course, we monitor constantly, it would just be a matter of following any trails that appear when you alert us. If you give me the details you hold on him – his name, any companies that you know he is involved with and so forth, I'll do some research and let you know if I turn anything up."

~

Marco sat at the café in the square in Fiesole that night, nursing a beer and trying to stave off the distressing memories that always intruded when he was confronted with the foul presence of Tommaso Rialo. That he was behind the supply of virtually all the illicit drugs in Tuscany was an open secret, but knowing something and proving it were two different things. A personal tragedy two years ago had sucked Marco into the underworld of Florentine addiction, face to face with organised crime and money laundering. Among the well to do of the city, cocaine was the drug of choice, the thing to be seen with, accessory to the rich and famous of the art scene. Polar opposites were the addicts lured in with cheap, even free, supplies of heroin; once hooked, the price went up and the quality down as the dealers mercilessly cut the drug with talcum or chalk dust.

She had been so full of life when they first met, a positive force that led Marco to dream that life after the intelligence services could indeed accommodate a loving partner and that trust was not, forever, beyond him. He had noticed the signs early on, the weight loss, the torpor, the bags under the eyes. She'd dismissed it as partying with her girlfriends, using heroin to come down from the cocaine high. Confrontation, coercion, pleading – nothing got through to her. He staked out her friend's flat and took on the dealer face to face; he won the particular battle that night but those higher up administered a beating to his girlfriend severe enough to place her in intensive care and a clear message to stay away was included for free.

Marco went to those who knew the scene from below the radar, his colleagues in intelligence. They knew Tommaso was the kingpin and that he had a sophisticated network of suppliers and dealers. That he laundered the money was a similar open secret but they had never come across someone so adept at covering his tracks. Soon after she recovered from her injuries, Marco's fiancée died from an overdose; the inquest heard that it was an unusually pure batch of heroin. Marco knew that it was a targeted assassination.

~

Taddeo called him the very next day. "I spoke with my colleagues and it turns out that several of us have been keeping an eye on *Signore* Rialo. We've come up with some interesting observations. Rather carelessly, he's created multiple tax identities. It's rather a basic error for someone so sophisticated but it makes it easier to track the different funding streams, something we're now actively pursuing. Perhaps he's getting complacent.

"There are several companies listed under Rialo's name. There's nothing necessarily sinister in that, but when you attempt to clarify the membership and composition of those companies it's very nebulous; that's another red flag.

"You're right with the multiple deposits too. We've altered the algorithm for pinging up deposits to accounts linked to Rialo and they have been fed repeatedly for many months now. This fits with placement, the first stage in money laundering.

"As we discussed, I focused on transactions involving Far East financial institutions and there are several. In particular, one of his companies has regular dealings with a bank in Singapore and there have been some U-turn transactions, which are always suspicious. That's when the money leaves here, is received in Singapore and very quickly a similar transaction passes the other way. It's often part of the layering process.

"Finally, we regularly compare the income of a suspect business with its competitors; when we did so we noticed two things. Tommaso Rialo's company involved in art restoration, run through Palazzo Moretti, has always earned vastly superior profits to the other competing companies and secondly, perhaps because of this, those competitors have, one by one, drifted away."

This was hugely encouraging thought Marco, who heaped fulsome praise on his colleague as he hung up. Now they had some ammunition to use against Tommaso, but he was very determined that when he took aim and fired he did not miss.

Eleanora Di Toledo
Florence, 1553

She had patiently bided her time. Involvement in the internecine world of Florentine politics had taught her that it was often necessary to play the waiting game. The Jesuit presence in the city was increasingly tolerated; Diego Laínez had been preaching here since 1547, but Cosimo had remained intransigent to the idea of them establishing a college. He stated that there simply was no appetite among the young people of Florence for this kind of education.

Then, two years ago, her patience had finally paid off. She had persuaded Cosimo to meet with Father Laínez. Her husband counted, among his many qualities, the possession of an open mind and, following a series of frank and open discussions, which both parties had thoroughly enjoyed, he had finally agreed to the establishment of a Jesuit college, but in Pisa rather than Florence. Although somewhat disappointed, Eleanora had long since learned to take small victories where she could find them and had offered grateful thanks to her husband for his magnanimity.

When it came to the practicalities, she agreed to share the cost for the project from her personal income. For the initial outlay, Cosimo contributed two hundred *scudi* whilst she contributed one hundred. On the one hand, she had simply believed this was the right thing to do, but, behind this, lay a conscious decision to demonstrate a growing independence from Cosimo.

Until now, her role had been envisaged as an extension of Cosimo – a wife and mother. She was celebrated, both amongst the people and in the iconography of the duchy, in terms of her fecundity and wealth. Now she yearned to be seen and recognised increasingly as a virtuous, capable woman, who made achievements on entirely her own merits.

And today, she had achieved one of her most glorious moments. Father Laínez had recently been called away as Papal envoy to the Council of Trent, with Father Elpidio Ugoletti arriving in his place. She had agreed to Ignatius of Loyola's request that she broker a meeting between Ugoletti and Cosimo, at which her husband had finally agreed to hand over the church of San Giovannino to the Order. The Jesuits finally had their college in Florence.

Chapter 17
Florence
May 2018

Marco strolled along Via dei Calzaiuoli, heading for Palazzo Vecchio. The excitement of chasing a criminal like Tommaso Rialo had him feeling alive in a way that had been missing from his life for years. What was it about him that necessitated confrontation as the central tenet of his life? His mother had died when he was young, leaving his father to raise him and his elder brother. Arlo had been a bright kid who, as soon as was feasible, took a scholarship and high tailed it to university in Milan. He'd graduated in pharmaceutical sciences and now worked in product development for Pfizer. Marco hadn't heard from him in over ten years.

His father was a strict disciplinarian, a factory worker in the textile industry. He approved of Marco's decision to pursue a career in the intelligence services, even if he secretly harboured doubts about the boy's academic potential. Sadly, he had died before he got the chance to see either of his boys graduating, a life given exclusively to the continuation of the family name. He would have been disappointed to know that his children had combined to destroy this ambition within a generation; Arlo was gay and Marco had decided there was no place for children in his admittedly jaundiced view of the world.

Being an intelligence operative did not lend itself well to intimate relationships and, even thirteen years later, he still found it difficult to trust anyone; that was the nature of the job he did. Making a living out of exposing corruption, lies and deceit wasn't always easy, but Marco had a keenly developed sense of right and wrong and consoled himself with the knowledge that, for every fraudster unmasked, there was at least one person whose life was made better. Take Giulia for example; he would never have suspected someone as well known and respected as her would be in bed with Tommaso Rialo. With a shiver, he hoped that was a figurative and not a literal analogy. Her husband deserved better. The opportunity was there though, he was frequently away dealing in the Far East, wasn't he? *The Far East.* Marco stopped and looked in the shop window he was passing. He saw a most unusual sight – his face was smiling. Sometimes his innate ability to see the worst in people paid dividends.

~

It was early evening and the Palazzo Vecchio was closed to visitors. Marco approached the glass door at the entrance to the ticket area and tapped his ring on the glass. A security guard raised his hand in salute, sauntered over and let him in. *"Ciao Marco. Come stai?"*

"Bene, bene. È Gianfranco qui?"

His friend nodded and gestured to him to go through. Marco knocked on a door at the far end of the passageway and entered, greeting his friend who was seated at an array of cameras displaying CCTV shots from around the building. The first courtyard, with the sculpture of the *putti* with the dolphin melded into a view of the massive Salone dei Quincecento, eerily empty of the normal throng of visitors. The tiny *studiolo* of Cosimo, a jewel box of painting, stucco and sculptures. The Apartments of the Elements, previously the quarters of Cosimo. The chambers of Eleanora, now sealed to the public as the long process of restoration got underway.

They exchanged pleasantries then Marco asked if he could see some of the recordings from the last few hours. Gianfranco's face fell; this was irregular and he feared getting into trouble if his supervisor found out. Marco took a bundle of banknotes from his pocket and peeled a twenty euro note off, looking enquiringly at his friend. He remained impassive; Marco smiled and peeled off another note. Gianfranco inclined his head towards the door and his colleague beyond. Marco laughed and peeled off two further bills. His friend smiled, clapped him on the shoulder and exited the room.

Marco sat down at the console and pulled up the feed from the camera located in the *camera verde,* the first of the chambers of Eleanora. He fast forwarded the recording, watching as restorers came and went, sometimes carrying packages or pieces of scaffolding. Soon he reached the point where a stream of workers exited, the final one being Tommaso Rialo, who locked the gate and pocketed the key. As he did so, he appeared to click a device on his key ring, akin to the remote locking device on a car alarm.

Marco checked the time; two hours ago. He then played the tape forward at speed until, suddenly, his eye was drawn to a fleeting blur of motion in the very corner of the screen. He continued forward and there it was again. And again. He flicked back and forward; the artefact appeared every thirteen minutes. He rewound to just before the moment it was due and played the tape at normal speed.

Seconds later, he laughed out loud. Either that mouse had a schedule like clockwork, or someone with a good knowledge of electronics was showing off.

Chapter 18
Florence
May 2018

The restoration process was swinging into its main phase. Within the apartments of Eleanora in the Palazzo Vecchio, a team of restorers were working on carefully erected scaffolding to commence the initial cleansing of Vasari's painted and gilded ceilings. The work required painstaking hours of lying motionless on one's back, trying to avoid dripping olive oil soap suds into ones eyes. It was akin to, albeit much less glamorous than, Michaelangelo's labours in painting the ceiling of the Sistine chapel.

In the confines of the *camera verde,* Tommaso was supervising the installation of the 3D scanners and Lidar mapping systems that would be used to create a replica of the Chapel of Eleanora, to be installed outside the apartments so that visitors could enjoy the splendours of Bronzino's jewel during its lengthy restoration. Thereafter, the chapel was to be permanently installed in the *cenacolo* where his 'Last Supper' was to be found.

The flatbed digital printer that would repeatedly overprint in perfect registration, allowing the replica to retain the surface complexity and characteristics of the original chapel walls, was located in an adjacent room, where restoration of the ceiling had been postponed until a later date. The printer would painstakingly reproduce the surface of the frescoes onto a flexible skin, which would then be mounted onto the lightweight aluminium frames from which the replica chapel would be constructed.

Tommaso had first seen the technology on a visit to the Valley of the Kings in Egypt, where they had created an exact facsimile of the burial chamber of Tutankhamen in a new building at the entrance to the Valley. He knew then that it was exactly what he required for his forthcoming project in Florence. His contract with the company who produced the equipment was convoluted. They had initially insisted on complete control of the operation, but he baulked at this, quoting a need for flexibility of timetables due to uncertainty over how degraded the frescoes would be; a degree of stabilisation would be required prior to the main reconstruction. In return for an enhanced schedule of payment, the suppliers ceded some control of operation back to Tommaso, accepting that the machines might lie dormant at times.

He busied himself in the work, liaising closely with the project director so that he could gain a working knowledge of the equipment. It kept his mind off Giulia's constant worrying and nagging; she seriously needed to calm herself or could prove to be a liability. Over the years she had carried out her part in his business dealings so efficiently that no one could have even begun to suspect, but she now appeared rattled and ill at ease. Now that Gio was gone, he would need her to step up to the plate, or be forced to find a way to replace her. Of course, that would mean silencing her, permanently, but – well, business was business…

Eleanora di Toledo
Siena, 1559

Sometimes war is not the only way, she reflected wryly, as they entered the city in victory. The Camollia gate in the north wall of Siena, facing Florence, bore the salutation *'COR MAGIS TIBI SEN PANDIT'*. 'Siena opens her heart to you more than this gate'. Hyperbole, thought Eleanora with a smile; I may be their Duchess now but they're not throwing themselves at my feet.

Cosimo had fought long and hard for control of this bitter enemy, his resolve strengthened by matters of a very personal nature. The opposing forces at the decisive Battle of Marciano, five long years hence, had been led by Piero Strozzi, scion of the family who were one of the Medici's long term combatants in Florence. Victory had been one of his sweetest, if not most decisive; the city had been under siege for a year thereafter before coming under the control of the Spanish ambassador of Charles V. It was only now that Spain and France had signed a peace treaty that he, as Spain's regional ally, could claim the city and finally end the republic of Siena.

They rode, side by side, locals paying respect to the royal couple as expected, but no more. The site of the Spanish citadel had been razed to the ground, with work well under way on the Medici fort of Santa Barbara which would replace it. The Spanish blood in Eleanora warmed slightly at this symbolic crushing of her homeland, but she knew her husband still showed her unwavering fidelity and respect. He acknowledged that she still felt Spanish at heart, talking with and writing to her courtiers in her native tongue and he accepted this, respectful of the efforts she had always made to converse in his native Italian tongue.

Having paused to inspect the building works, the couple and their retinue rode on, through the narrow streets. Riders ahead cleared the streets of pedestrians, somewhat roughly thought Eleanora, who preferred sweetness to force as a means of gaining respect. They rode into Piazza Tolomei, where city officials had erected a large fictive bronze relief depicting Juno, intended to refer to Eleanora's authority and intercession, her role in easing the weight of Cosimo's rule. She was pleased at this tribute to her virtues and talents as a leader. And yet, beside it was a marble figure representing Cybele, mother of the gods, alluding to Eleanora's fertility. She sighed with frustration, accepting that, no matter how respected she became, there would always be a strata of society which regarded her as simply the progenitor of male Medici heirs.

Soon they were off and riding again, keen to get out of the saddle and rest. Everything in Siena sloped down, so it seemed, along streets whose towering houses nearly touched overhead, down towards the massive shell-shaped Piazza del Campo, into which they now rode.

It was a magnificent sight. The *Fonte Gaia,* with its statues by Jacopo della Quercia, stood immediately in front of them; they paused to allow their dust covered horses to drink. Ahead stood the Palazzo Pubblico, previously the seat of the Republican government but now home to Cosimo's civic administrators. The *Capella di Piazza* fronted the building, topped by the spectacular *Torre del Mangia.* To their left was their destination, the Palazzo Sansedoni, home to one of the city's most prominent families, keen to ingratiate themselves with their new Duke and Duchess by providing lavish hospitality.

The head of the household met the party at the Palazzo's gate, bowing low. Dispatching servants to stable the horses and billet the men, he gestured for his honoured guests to enter his home.

"Thank you, *Signore,* for your warm welcome. Before we wash off the dust, I would care to show my lady the beauty of our city. Please take us inside the Palazzo Pubblico and then up the Tower."

Sansedoni sketched a deep bow. "With honour, your majesties."

They crossed the *piazza* and entered the Palazzo, passing through the internal courtyard with its gilded tin statue of the she wolf feeding the twins, symbol of the city, believed to be founded by Senius and

Aschius, sons of Remus. Inside was the large hall of government, with its imposing fresco of 'Maesta', by Simone Martini. Eleanora closed her eyes for a moment in silent devotion.

Cosimo, more akin to his nature, now stood next door in front of Ambrogio Lorenzetti's 'Allegory of Good and Bad Government'. He smiled. "Propaganda and free advice have been available for over two hundred years, I see".

Eleanora joined him, taking his arm. "You need no advice, husband. You rule wisely and with compassion."

He smiled at her. "Were it otherwise, would you tell me?"

"Most certainly. That is one of the roles of a caring and loving wife."

Sansedoni was warmed by this unusual display of public affection. He had heard that the new ruler of his city was a fair and just lord and hope rose in his heart that this was true. He gestured to the regal couple to precede him on the long climb up the tower.

~

The view was magnificent. Siena spread before them, a surprisingly small city, the buildings packed in as if space were at a premium. The shadow of the tower was cast across the Piazza and over the buildings beyond. The walls of the city seemed as much designed to herd all the dwellings of the city together as to keep invaders out. The massive cathedral complex with its belfry stood just below and to their left, whilst more distant was the austere façade and square, gothic *campanile* of Santa Maria dei Servi. In a surprisingly tender gesture, Cosimo took his wife's hand. He was very conscious of that moment how fortunate his life had been and offered up a silent prayer for continued health and happiness.

Chapter 19
Florence
May 2018

Marco's final port of call that day was to the *Grande Oriente d'Italia* lodge where he frequently met with his current source inside the AISI. The secure, confidential nature of the lodge made it the ideal venue in which to hold the very sensitive communications that passed between the two. Marco often acted as a conduit through which information from the community fed into the intelligence network; today he was hoping for a reversal of flow. Gianluca appeared relaxed and not at all surprised by his line of inquiry. "As you can imagine, there's no tears shed over the passing of Gio Rialo. He was a nasty, petty criminal, with none of the intelligence and gravitas that his father possesses. Word is that Gio had gotten wind of a very big deal in the offing and was stupid enough to lean on his father to cut him a piece of the action. There's only one way that was ever going to end. Daddy asked one of his more muscular acquaintances to enlighten Gio and teach him the wisdom of silence, but muscles got rather over enthused and it ended badly – both for Gio and for him. It's hard to swim with your pockets full of boulders."

"My client's father has landed the starring role of prime suspect. There's no way he did it, but Esposito has him nicely fitted up and Tommaso's providing a couple of supporting actors, so I think he's balls deep in trouble."

Gianluca shook his head. "Perhaps the fact that Esposito couldn't find his own arsehole with the lights out might come to his rescue."

"I'm also interested in the demise of Danieli Restauro and other art restorers recently. I've had a tip off that they're being destroyed from the inside. Apparently someone is switching out genuinely sourced, authentic paints, to be used in the illicit reproduction market, and substituting substandard pigments which deteriorate after the work is returned in its restored state. The company is then brought into disrepute."

Gianluca smiled, appreciative of the ingenuity of the scheme. "Sometimes I wish I was half as smart as the bastards we're trying to catch! I'll see if there's a link with the other companies which are floundering or have already gone out of business. Anything else?"

Marco smiled. "Since you asked so nicely, there is actually. See if you can dig up anything on shipments to the Far East, anything which does or could contain works of art. And look to see if there's any evidence of a dealer by the name of Antonio Bianchi working out in that part of the world."

"*Nessun problema.* So, how is life treating you? We don't see much of you down here in the big city. You too good for us now you're up in the rarified air of Fiesole?"

Marco smiled. "Not at all. Just too much in love with my own company. We should grab a beer sometime for sure?"

"You still playing handball?" Marco had represented his country in the sport for over five years; his great regret was that the team had not managed to qualify for either the 1996 or 2000 Olympics.

He laughed. "You kidding? It's a young man's game, I'd probably collapse. Best I can do is a jog along the river of an evening or the occasional spot of rowing; Gianfranco is a member of the *Societa Cannottieri.*"

"Well, definitely call me and arrange that beer. I'll get back to you as soon as I've got any information for you." Gianluca raised a hand in farewell.

Marco returned the salutation and left the lodge. He knew he wouldn't be calling Gianluca for a beer, a run or to go rowing; he never took up Gianfranco's offers anyway and his friend had now given up asking. The solitary life was Marco's choice now. He'd let one person into his life and look how that had ended.

Eleanora di Toledo
Palazzo Vecchio
Florence, 1560

She sits through the latest meeting with *Signore* Vasari, wishing (not for the first time) that he was not quite so loquacious. She believes she has made her views abundantly clear, but the artist appears unnecessarily anxious that her views should be in alignment with those of Cosimo.

"I can assure you, *signore,* that the Grand Duke is entirely cognisant of my choices and in complete agreement with them. You may proceed as we have discussed."

Vasari inclines his head respectfully. "I am honoured, your majesty. But perhaps if I could show you these preliminary sketches…"

She stifles a sigh, gesturing encouragement instead with a flick of the wrist.

"We agreed that each room would focus on an event from the life of a famous woman to whom the room is dedicated. This event occupies a large central panel, with smaller soffits around it. A frieze runs below each ceiling. For the *Sala della Sabine.."*

In his charcoal sketches, Sabine women intercede in combat between their Roman husbands and Sabine male relatives, while the frieze contains allegories of peace, fame, fortitude and charity all represented as women. She nods in approval and he sets the sketches aside.

"And now the *Sala di Esther..".* Esther kneels before her husband who grants her plea, whilst the frieze tells the rest of Esther's story.

"The *Sala di Penelope..".* Penelope sits at her loom amidst other women spinning; the frieze shows Ulysses' adventures and four virtues represented as women.

"Finally, the *Sala di Guadralda..*". She stops him; the tale of this Florentine maiden is unfamiliar to her. He quickly informs her, then demonstrates the maiden confronting Emperor Otto IV and her father, while Flora lounges in foreground. The frieze alternates views of Florence with female representation of four virtues

"Together, your majesty, as we desire, these images construct a very positive image of you as a force at the heart of the state."

She smiles, her heart swelling with pride. Her iconography, until now, celebrated her fecundity, her virtue, her role as wife. She was normally depicted as Juno, focusing again on her fecundity, serenity, piety, wealth, role as a duchess and as a wife. She had no will in any of this. She was seen as an object of admiration rather than emulation. While there was absolutely nothing wrong with being admired, it was because of her position as Cosimo's wife, not as a worthy individual in her own right. Now she wants to be seen differently, to be exemplified as exercising her willed choices in the cardinal virtues and in her public role. These new rooms will celebrate her participation in the establishment, governance, economic well-being and peacefulness of the duchy.

She believes that women are as capable of the four cardinal virtues as men, and that virtue and the ability to rule comes as naturally to women as men. This new decorative scheme will focus on her power derived from moral action, portraying her as a wise, valiant, chaste, prudent 'Donna Regia', a worthy earthly counterpart to Cosimo.

Chapter 20
Florence
May 2018

Lucrezia was struggling to act normally around Giulia, feeling hurt at the betrayal she and her father had suffered. Her life had been sheltered up until now, she realised, surrounded by people who had her best interests at heart, who behaved with dignity and fairness. She was completely unprepared for being used, manipulated and lied to like this. Ironically, the fact that she had no concept of how to strike back was beneficial in the challenging task of swallowing her fury and acting as if nothing had changed.

But inside, she *felt* different. Her sense of frustration at being let down by her father had been complicated by the loyalty she naturally felt towards him, which precluded even a scathing verbal attack. There were no such restraints on the range of responses available to her to counter the calculated cruelty and deception visited upon her by the Rialo's and Giulia. She began to foment vendettas of revenge, incubating her hatred silently.

She continued to have regular contact with Marco, who stressed the importance of maintaining a sense of normality. He wanted her to feed another prompt to Tommaso by the covert communication channel they had surreptitiously established. Jeffrey was due in front of the prosecutor in less than twenty four hours.

Over breakfast, Lucrezia asked if Giulia could show her some of the works by female artists in the Uffizi. Giulia, looking tired, agreed somewhat hesitantly and the two set off on the short walk.

"There are surprisingly few works by women in the Uffizi, and many of those actually hang in the Vasari corridor, which, as you know, is closed to the public. The Pitti Palace has many more works – over sixty between the Palatine and the Modern Art gallery, but I know you're keen to see Artemisia, and the Uffizi has her most famous work. What do you know about 'Judith Slaying Holofernes'?"

Lucrezia knew this painting well; she had admired its strength. "There are six versions, the Uffizi one being painted in 1620. It's very reminiscent of Caravaggio's depiction of the same scene at the Palazzo Barberini in Rome."

"Yes, I agree. Her father was a painter, very influenced by Caravaggio and she certainly picked up his style. She lived here in Florence from 1614 to 1620 and Grand Duke Cosimo II was a patron."

At the gallery, Giulia was, once again, able to use her influence to bypass the interminable queues and soon they stood before the imposing work. There was an intense savagery in the work as two servants, one clad in a mustard coloured dress, struggled to overcome the man, grabbing his beard to expose his throat, which she slashed with a sword. It was, if anything, more brutal than the Caravaggio work, and stirred something deep in Lucrezia. She chose to verbalise it, sensing that Giulia would not.

"Is it true that this work was painted in response to her rape?"

Giulia considered her reply carefully. "We know she was raped in 1611 and, most unusually for the time, testified against her attacker in court. One can certainly read her painting as a revenge work, but I prefer to take a wider view, that she enjoyed depicting powerful women. She was certainly entitled to do so; she was regarded as one of the most progressive and expressive painters of her generation and was the first female member of the Accademia di Arte del Disegno."

Giulia indicated a portrait adjacent to the work. "This is her depiction of 'Saint Catherine of Alexandria'."

Lucrezia studied the picture – it showed a serious face and a strong, blocky presence. This was a depiction of character not beauty, a somehow deeply feminine representation of gravitas delivered from a position of sisterhood. The painting resonated strongly with Lucrezia's new found tenacity in the face of adversity.

"There's a major exhibition of Artemisia's work in the National Gallery in London in 2020," announced Giulia. "We've been asked to draw up a potential list of complementary works by female artists of the same period. I'm thinking of including Lavinia Fontana – have you come across her?"

Lucretia shook her head.

"She came from Bologna and is often thought of as the first female career artist in Europe, as she relied on commissions for her livelihood. She also managed to be the mother of eleven children while pursuing a successful career! This is an unusual pice, a self portrait painted in oils on copper. And this is a more traditional subject, a *'Noli me tangere.'*"

Lucrezia peered closely at the circular self portrait; it was small, merely six inches in diameter, and very dark in colour, but showed a very self possessed elegant woman, clad in a fine gown with a high ruff collar, seated at a desk, pen in hand. The work was prominently signed. "She appears very self-confident, both in her visage and the flourish with which the work has been signed."

The 'Noli me Tangere' was a fascinating work. Lucrezia remembered (from somewhere) that the scriptural text had Mary mistaking the resurrected Jesus for the gardener, but had never seen the text so literally transposed into art. Jesus was depicted wearing a coarse, belted smock, a wide-brimmed straw hat and carrying a long handled spade. Lucrezia knew that the work was visually representative of the theology of the time, representing Christ as planting the flourishing seeds of virtue, but the appearance could have come across as farcical. Instead, Lucrezia found its naivety charming and moving.

As they left the gallery, Lucrezia was buoyed by the evidence of women presenting as successful, bold and innovative creators in a world still very much dominated by male artists, patrons and rulers. She thought back a few days to her visit to the Palazzo Vecchio and the chambers of Eleanora di Toledo, a duchess who had risen to earn respect and wield power in her own right. But then, she cast a sideways glance at Giulia, striding along confidently, showing no evidence of the deceit and cruelty hidden in her heart. It was all she could do not to turn and walk away. She must be strong, but for how long could she maintain the charade?

Eleanora di Toledo
Death
San Lorenzo
Florence, 28th December 1562

Amidst all the feelings he is experiencing today, it chafes him that the most pressing at the moment is that of being too warm. Cosimo wears a heavy black gown over his long, fur-lined mourning dress of grey damask, embroidered in gold and silver. Around the baldacchino are a hundred men in long black cloaks and black berets, with veils covering their heads and necks; he wonders if they also are sweating with the heat of thousands of candles. The walls of the basilica of San Lorenzo are covered in heavy black hangings decorated with skeletons and the Toledo coat of arms, adding to the oppressive feeling of the occasion. The casket, containing the body of his beloved Eleanora, sits under the baldacchino covered with a pall of cloth-of-gold, edged with black velvet and decorated with the Medici-Toledo arms.

Outside, a large crowd has gathered to bid farewell to their Duchess, gratified by being offered a civic holiday to mark the occasion. They listen in hushed reverence to the Latin oration delivered by Piero Vettori. The mass is sung by Bishop de'Nerli; many in the crowd outside genuflect and respond to the litany.

Cosimo runs back through the previous few months in his mind, cursing his luck but also blaming himself for actions he would readily undo if he had the time again. In October, he and Eleanora had taken Giovanni, Garzia and Ferdinando to Pisa; they went via Siena, the Maremma and Livorno to Pisa. If only he had avoided that pestilential swamp, the Maremma! Eleanora and two boys had contracted malaria, Giovanni becoming ill first and dying in Livorno on November 20th.

The rest of the family had travelled on to Pisa, seeking the advice of Eleanora's physician, Andrea Pasquali, who a mere six months previously had treated her for similar ailments in Pisa; she had made a magical recovery. Sadly, this time the outcome was disastrous. Garzia died on December 12th and his beloved mother five days later. Cosimo had held her hand as, weakened by tuberculosis and wracked by fever, her life slipped away, comforted by the presence of her Jesuit confessor, Father Francisco Estrada.

The deaths of three members of his family in such quick succession is a body blow to Cosimo. Although still in shock, he is now of a mind to pass leadership of the duchy to Ferdinando. The funerals of both sons had taken place quickly, and with a minimum of fuss, but the grand duchess, the woman to whom he had remained faithful and devoted all their married lives, deserves a magnificent send off.

Eleanora's body had been quickly prepared for transfer to Florence and burial, although fear of contagion from malaria and tuberculosis meant that the corpse had not embalmed. Her body arrived in Florence in a closed casket on December 20th, draped in black velvet marked with a Red Cross, accompanied by a large group of mounted courtiers bearing one hundred and fifty torches. She was met by the first citizens of the city on horseback and the casket carried to San Lorenzo by, among others, her son Giulio. They stopped at the Duomo en route to allow the citizens of her city to pay homage.

In San Lorenzo her casket was displayed in front of the high altar, where she and Cosimo had married twenty three years previously, while high mass was sung. The casket was then deposited in the old sacristy, to whence it will return in a few moments for her body to be interred in the family crypts.

Cosimo knows she will never be forgotten, and not only by him and their children. As a patron of the arts, she has left an indelible mark, with commissions and buildings which will preserve her memory for millennia. She had made her will just the day before she died, leaving most of her estate to Cosimo but making a bequest to the Jesuits – two hundred scudi per annum for their church and school of San Giovannino. She also gave a legacy of one thousand scudi a year in perpetuity towards the building and support of a convent, Santissima Concezione. Particularly in her later years, his beloved Eleanora has been celebrated as a powerful and successful, virtuous woman in her own right, emerging from his shadow to take her rightful place in the duchy. Her benevolence will bless the lives of women for generations to come. He smiles as he reflects on how much pleasure that would have brought his beloved wife,

Chapter 21
Florence
May 2018

Jeffrey sat in the room, head bowed as if in silent prayer. Lucrezia stood at the door, uncertain as to what to say, what to do? What feelings were bubbling up inside him; relief at being released or guilt at using the lies of a woman to his own ends? He had always been in possession of a strong moral compass and the fact that lies and corruption had imprisoned him in the first place would not justify his resorting to similar means to secure his freedom. He now faced the prospect of having to contact his wife, as there was a good chance the case would make the news media. He baulked at the prospect of being on the receiving end of a stream of invective from a woman still reeling from the shock of his deceit.

"Are you ready dad?"

He looked up, face strong and composed. "Yes, I'm ready. The world doesn't always play fair and it's been a hard lesson that sometimes you need to stand up to it. I'm not going to let our marriage die, I'm going to fight. I'll apologise, just once, then all my energies go into making things right. For all three of us."

Lucrezia gave him a hug, then snuck out of the room, leaving him to steel himself for what lay ahead. He dialled the house in Oxford, half expecting to have the phone slammed down on him. She answered, sounding even more distant than the geographical miles that separated them.

"Marie, it's me. Please don't hang up, it's about Lucrezia."

"My god, what's happened?"

"She's ok, I'm in Florence with her now. She's been through an ordeal, we both have, but I need you to listen to me while I explain. For her sake, not mine."

Over the next fifteen minutes, he laid out the convoluted story of all that had happened in just a few short days. Somewhat to his surprise, his wife listened in silence – he even began to wonder if the line had been cut. When he reached the part where Marco's friend supplied him with a false alibi, he heard a snort of derision down the phone and braced himself for the onslaught. It never came.

"Marie, I'm so sorry. For what I did those years ago. But not for this. I did what I needed to do for our daughter."

Silence. He waited, then was about to speak again, when he heard her reply, soft and sad. "God knows you've enough to apologise for, Jeffrey. But you're right, not for this. You were there when our daughter needed you. In fact, until recently, you always were, even when….you know. She needed you and you went to save her. And I thank you for that."

He was close to tears; shame and gratitude was a confusing mixture. "Marie, I …"

"Not now, Jeffrey, please." Surprisingly gently. "When you're sure she's safe, come home. Then we'll meet and talk. I've been too hurt to listen but I need to understand why you did what you did. Perhaps I never will, but you've earned enough respect to entitle you to be heard."

"I don't deserve…"

"We both need to decide what you deserve. Only you can decide if you live with shame all your life or forgive yourself and move on. I can't do that for you. I haven't had the time or to be honest the inclination to decide if you deserve my forgiveness, but it needs answering if I am to move on, either with or without you." She hung up.

Jeffrey was weeping softly now. Lucrezia, who had been hovering outside the door came in and sat beside him on the bed. He raised his eyes and shook his head. "I don't deserve her forgiveness."

Lucrezia smiled. "It's hers to give dad. What you need to do is forgive yourself. If you regard what you did as wrong, then all you can do, all anyone can do, is apologise and try to make a better job next time. You've always been there for me, never more so than now, and I love you very much."

Chapter 22
Florence
May 2018

Jeffrey sat with Marco in the bar in Fiesole. "You can be a big help if you do this, Jeffrey. I'm too well known in the *oltrarno* ; if I'm seen sniffing around then Tommaso will be alerted and people will be threatened into silence or worse. Here are the two people I've set up to meet with you – their addresses are on the back of the photos. Just chat about the gossip doing the rounds and listen out for any word on Tommaso."

Jeffrey took the pictures and studied the faces of the men he hoped would provide information leading them closer to the misdemeanours of the Rialos. He had never countenanced any kind of subterfuge before; he was a man of scrupulous morals but now he was in a game where the rules were set by others and he was determined to play his part.

~

Later that afternoon, he strolled along the small streets of the artisans' district, taking in the sights and sounds of the men at work. He turned into Piazza Santo Spirito and immediately recognised the wizened, mahogany coloured face of his first contact. Jeffrey strolled up to the bar, ordered a bottle of *grappa* and two glasses and sat down with the aged worthy, pouring him a glass by way of introduction. The man raised it in salute, downed it in one, fixed Jeffrey with an inquiring eye then smiled toothlessly as his glass was refilled. "*Salute*," he croaked in greeting.

"Marco's a good man to have on your side," he began. "He's right to be looking at Tommaso for that poor girl who got attacked." Jeffrey fought back his rage; concentrate, keep calm and do your job. He asked a few preliminary questions that Marco had suggested would break the ice. After running the rule over mutual acquaintances and decrying the current woes of his beloved Fiorentina, the old artisan huddled closer, glanced around in an overtly conspiratorial way and whispered, "There's a run on old frames, panels and canvasses. Never a huge amount at a time, but the same faces keep appearing. Paying good money too. There are a few of the customers that I've heard are definitely a part of Tommaso's circle; it seems like everything gravitates back to his orbit, doesn't it?"

Jeffrey poured him another glass; lubrication usually proved fruitful at times like these.

"Did you hear that Luigi and Paulo got paid off? Looks like Danieli Restauro is going out of business."

Jeffrey knew about the establishment; they were one of the few big private restorers left in Florence. "No, I hadn't heard. What's the story?"

The man leaned in again, reeking of *grappa,* revelling in being the portent of doom. "Some big scandal they're trying to keep under wraps. Apparently they were using cheap alternative paints to skim some money off a restoration contract but then the colours went wrong and when the owner of the work asked them to redo it, the fakes wouldn't come off, so the work is ruined. The proprietor was dismissed by the committee of management but the story's gonna break in the papers and…" He shrugged in the universal language of 'game over'.

In full flow, the grizzled veteran rattled on. "No one was sorry to hear about his son, a real wrong'un that. He'd crapped on a few of us down here, coming over all high and mighty. My friend got 'nicely asked' to grass up that girl's father they've arrested but he wouldn't do it – says he couldn't live with his conscience and the worry about perjuring himself. He reckons it's gonna come out that old Tommaso had a hand in his son's death, tried to teach the boy a lesson but it all went wrong. Peruzzi, who they fished out of the Arno the other night, always was a bit heavy handed mind you."

Jeffrey felt a huge debt of gratitude to the man who had, bravely, resisted implicating him in Gio's death. He felt like he was trying to assemble the pieces of a puzzle and finally getting a sense of the picture he was trying to recreate. In isolation, none of the nuggets he had gleaned today would come anywhere near building a case against Tommaso Rialo, but if he could somehow pull them all together and take aim…He decided to pull harder on a couple of those threads.

~

Luigi Marconi was clearly angry and welcoming of the chance to sound off about his dismissal. Jeffrey felt a twinge of guilt about posing as an insurance agent for the owner of the damaged work, but that didn't stop him investing his very best acting skills in the role.

"I *felt* there was something wrong right away," Luigi grumbled, "you can tell a pigment by its feel and smell and this just seemed *off*. But I checked the container and the shipping manifest and it all checked out – same container, invoices from the usual supplier. Some bastard must have replaced the genuine paint with a cheap alternative. But why? They might make a few euros selling the paint on or even doing some freelancing, but the risks don't seem worth it. It's the ones who made that switch that should be paying with their jobs, not us poor bastards who got fooled and were trying to do an honest job. But they can't follow the paper trail and locate the source of the breach, so out we go." He shook his head, clearly disgusted by the miscarriage of justice visited upon him.

"It's not the first such incident either," he continued, "although that one, last year, was a tapestry. After the repair, the owner noticed the replacement threads fading in the sunlight - shouldn't have hung the thing in the sunlight anyway but however – and when she kicked off, same thing; cheap Chinese threads in the original packaging, the proper materials long gone."
He threw up his arms in a final gesture of surrender.

"I mean, you'd think someone was deliberately out to get us shut down!"

'Yes', thought Jeffrey, 'that's *exactly* what I was thinking.'

Grand Duke Francesco I
Palazzo Pitti,
Florence, 1565

He preferred living here in the palace. Ever since Cosimo had stepped down, passing power to him, the family had enjoyed living here as their main residence. Francesco believed he had performed well as regent, retaining the affection and loyalty of his citizens that his father had striven to achieve. Aware of the importance of a strategic marriage, he had chosen Joanna of Austria, from the House of Habsburg, daughter of Ferdinand, Holy Roman Emperor. He was looking forward to the forthcoming nuptials.

He still missed his mother. She, along with his brothers Garzia and Giovanni, had caught malaria in that pestilential pit of Pisa three years ago; their deaths, one after the other, had been hammer blows even to the staunch Medici family.

His mother had bought the palace sixteen years ago, despite some misgivings about its rather austere appearance. The rusticated façade was certainly less elegant than that of the Palazzo Medici, and the three-times-repeated series of seven arched apertures gave it an air of a Roman aqueduct, but she had been rather charmed by the *alla'Antica* appearance. *Signore* Fanchelli had a certain style; Brunelleschi had taught him well. Cosimo, however, who at times took on the attitude of a caged animal, had called for more space (always more space!) and engaged *Signore* Vasari to build a whole new block behind the façade.

Personally, Eleanora was always more interested in the gardens, laid out on the hill behind the palace. Sadly, Niccolo Tribolo had died within a year of her appointing him, but she had been happy with *Signore* Ammanati's efforts as replacement. Currently he was beginning work on a reservoir supplying water to the *palazzo* which would be located in the north corner of the gardens and around which he planned a spectacular *grotte grande*. He was also designing the courtyards behind the palace which would form a pleasing link between the apartments and the gardens.

She would have been slightly bemused by Francesco's latest project, to link the *palazzo* with the Palazzo Vecchio by means of a covered overhead walkway. Vasari was nothing if not creative and industrious; it was a minor miracle that he had completed the whole project in a mere five months. Such was his haste that, while the Manelli family were vacillating about the request to move their *torre,* he had simply built round it!

From the *palazzo,* the corridor passed over houses on the *oltrarno* then actually through the church of Santa Felicita. A window in the wall allowed the family the luxury of taking mass in private from within the confines of the passageway. Then the corridor passed over the Ponte Vecchio, from the centre of which a window afforded beautiful views of the Arno towards the Ponte Santa Trinita. Eleanora had believed it to be the most beautiful of all Florence's bridges; he liked to picture her lingering here taking in the view. Thankfully, at his insistence, they had now moved that stinking meat market off the bridge below! The goldsmiths were a marked improvement in his opinion.

Then a sharp turn along the *lungarno* and over a bridge took Francesco to work in the Uffizi, free from the attention, respectful or otherwise, of his citizens as well as the vagaries of the Florentine climate. A shorter corridor from the Uffizi led to the Palazzo Vecchio, opening in the *camera verde* of his mother's personal suite of rooms, still left as it was, partly in tribute to her, partly due to both him and his father remaining in mourning for her. If his own marriage proved to be to a woman as charming, majestic and quietly determined as his mother, he would count himself fortunate indeed.

Chapter 23
Florence
May 2018

As soon as the restorers had departed for the night, and Tommaso had locked the gate, the door from the Vasari corridor opened and two figures clad in black, sprang into action. They began to switch on the array of scanners and printers in the apartments, waiting until the impressive range of machinery was up and running, quietly humming in anticipation.

One of the figures took his flashlight and disappeared back into the corridor. It still had an air redolent of dampness, despite the fact that they had been opening it now every day for a week. Moving to the sixth picture in line on the left hand wall, the man slipped it off the wall and retraced his steps to the *camera verde*. Walking through to the adjacent room, more brightly illuminated, he joined his colleague at a work surface erected on two trestle legs which had previously been stashed in the corner. Carefully placing the painting face down on a felt coverlet, he gently prised out the pins which retained the stretcher frame and lifted it free from the main frame of the work. Taking up the canvas thus liberated, he carefully placed it upright on a support, using a spirit level to ensure it was completely centred, vertically and horizontally; this prevented reflections from the surface hindering the next step. He then began the exhaustive process of panoramic composite photography, taking hundreds of overlapping high resolution images from a single viewpoint several metres from the painting. Even for a small canvas like this, it would take him over an hour.

When he was finished, he began the process of uploading his images to the computer. His colleague now moved the Lucida 3D scanner into place and began to obtain the necessary data from the surface of the work, revealing the complexity of the paintwork. As he scanned, the data input was processed to create a greyscale depth map image, displayed on a monitor. The computer now began to integrate the data streams, transforming them into a rich textural recreation of the surface of the painting. The software was stitching together the photos and the

3D data, laying the colour information on top of the relief information, to give a multilayered file.

Now the technician transferred the data to a printer which used the very latest elevated printing technology and, layer by layer, slowly built up a high resolution relief surface. The men were relaxed; they had carried out this whole process every night for the last five nights and were, by now, completely *au fait* with the cutting edge technology. Tonight saw them completing their task of assembling the set of six paintings expected by their client.

When the printing was completed, they poured liquid silicon over the surface, waiting for it to dry before carefully removing the flexible mould thus created. This mould was then cast in acrylic reinforced gesso and, at last, they had a faithful physical reproduction of the surface of the original painting.

As one man powered down the scanner and packed away the digital camera, his partner took the cast and placed it on the flatbed printer, fastidiously lining up the margins with the borders of the colour reproduction contained inside. With the touch of a button, the printer quietly began to faithfully reconstruct the priceless work of art.

It took half an hour to finish the task. When the printer had run its program, the finished reproduction, carefully reinstalled in its frame, was rehung in the corridor. The men toasted a long but successful evening with some *grappa* from a hip flask. The reproductions would pass even a close inspection, in the unlikely event that someone from the Uffizi decided to check on the collection in the Vasari corridor which, let's face it, had been pretty much locked up and forgotten about for years. The forgers in their rooms could have as much time as they needed with the originals before they returned with a fully painted forgery to rehang in the original frame.

They packaged the original painting carefully; it would be removed tomorrow as part of the normal comings and goings from the restoration site. Now they would take their time going along the Vasari corridor and exiting into the Boboli gardens; there were no cameras to worry about and plenty of places to lie low until the gardens opened and they could saunter out like a couple of tourists. Soon they would be handsomely rewarded for their efforts.

Chapter 24
Florence
May 2018

Jeffrey sat anxiously in the waiting room, studying the faces of his fellow patients, who were deep in worrying thoughts about their afflictions. His was a completely different type of fear. He was about to step even further beyond a line which he had been reluctant to cross in the first place, one where he used deceit and manipulation to further his own ends. How far would he need to pursue this – where, if ever, would he stop and say 'enough, no further'? The deep hatred he felt towards the man who had violated his daughter and simply expected to get away with it was driving him to actions which he would have found unconscionable merely days ago but his love as a father was an even more powerful determinant of his actions.

Dr. Riccardi came into the waiting room and called, 'Mr. Johnson'. Without waiting to see if anyone responded, she turned on her heels and strode into the consulting room. By the time Jeffrey had entered the room, she was seated behind a large desk, head down, writing on a piece of paper. As he waited in vain to be asked to take a seat, he studied the array of degrees and diplomas which decorated the wall behind her; obviously none was for bedside manner. Imagining how uncomfortable Lucrezia must have felt in the presence of this dismissive woman, he took a seat and sat back in the chair, prepared to wait as long as it took. He was feeling strangely calm now.

After a few moments, the doctor looked up over the top of her glasses, as if surprised to find a patient waiting there. "How can I help you, sir?" she asked sullenly.

Jeffrey waited, deliberately, before replying. "It's about my daughter, actually."

She frowned, clearly irritated. "Is she with you?"

Jeffrey played it with a straight bat. "No, she isn't."

Dr. Riccardi threw her arms wide in a sarcastic gesture. She was making this much easier than Jeffrey had anticipated. "Then I fail to see how I can assist you?"

"You can tell me about your examination at the police station the other day. The young woman you examined who had been sexually assaulted?"

She sat back, clearly disconcerted. "I'm sorry but I'm unable to discuss cases with anyone other than the patient, due to rules of confidentiality. Please leave."

She stood. Jeffrey didn't. "Well then, if you're not prepared to talk you can listen. You were negligent in your duties. I have evidence which can prove it. And I'm prepared to report you to the medical authorities. Now will you sit and listen?"

Her mouth hung open in disbelief. For a full minute she stood motionless then slowly sat down in her chair. Her eyes watched Jeffrey like a hawk. But he felt nothing like prey. He was in control here and she knew it. "Your report of your examination of my daughter stated that any abrasions present were minor and caused by her scratching herself. You know that is fictitious and, as such, in clear breach of your ethical duties, especially in a criminal investigation."

She bristled, adopting a defensive posture. "Those were my clear and unequivocal findings and I stand by them."

Jeffrey steeled himself for the part he had been most uncomfortable with. When it came, he felt not the slightest qualm. "As soon as she was released, I took my daughter for a further medical examination. Even then, nearly twenty four hours later, the doctor found clear signs that were consistent with non-consensual sex. I have a report to that effect in my possession."

How easy it had become to lie. Of course, his strategy was founded on never having to produce such a fictitious report.

"In addition, the swabs you took in evidence never reached the laboratory for analysis. Can you enlighten me regarding that?"

"I passed them to the custody sergeant, who signed for their receipt. There should be a clear data trail from there through the transport company to the laboratory."

"And who was the custody sergeant?"

She opened her desk drawer and leafed through a file, eventually producing a carbon copy of a receipt. "I believe this is what you are looking for…"

Jeffrey took the paper and confirmed the signatory; one Luigi Esposito.

"I'm going to ask you to think carefully about what I say next. Intelligence services are investigating Detective Esposito and about to bring charges of corruption against him. Those charges will extend to anyone who willingly complied with him. Anyone who was forced under duress to assist him, and who will testify to that, will be exempt from prosecution. In light of that knowledge, do you have anything to tell me about your examination of my daughter?"

She sat, head bowed for a moment. When she raised her head, there was a defeated look in her eyes. "When he called me in, Detective Esposito advised me that the assailant in the case was Tommaso Rialo and that I should produce a report casting doubt on his guilt. I immediately knew that was unethical and told him so, but he advised me that if my report implicated Rialo then he would let him know that I had done so. I suspect you have become aware of the average life expectancy of those who cross Tommaso Rialo…"

There was a time when Jeffrey would have felt sorry for the doctor, caught in an impossible situation, but that time had passed. He rose to leave; as he reached the door, he heard the doctor utter a final defiant challenge. "I'll deny that in court if I have to.."

Jeffrey strode on, the voice recorder tucked safely in his jacket pocket.

Chapter 25
Florence
May 2018

Lucrezia had never imaging life spying on someone else. Due to extreme patience and self control, she believed that Giulia did not yet know that they were monitoring her conversations. But Marco was keen to track her movements and had asked Lucrezia, whenever possible, to discreetly follow her.

That morning, Giulia had stated she was visiting the Palazzo and Lucrezia claimed she would just prefer a lazy morning at home. As Giulia left, she quietly slipped out and dropped into a position a hundred or so metres behind, where she could avoid detection. Giulia wandered through the streets towards the Santa Maria Novella quarter before stopping and, using a key, entering an unmarked building.

Giulia opened the door and entered the room, locking the door behind her. The lack of windows gave the room a claustrophobic feel but the gentle hiss of recycled air removed some of the oppression. Bright strip lights illuminated the twin easels on which sat the original oil work and its partly completed facsimile.

The artist sat applying layers of oil paint to the panel, cut from wood sourced from the appropriate period in the seventeenth century. The design had been sketched out as an under drawing and it now remained to build up the layers of impasto to replicate the three dimensional structure of the panel. Samples of the original pigments had been carefully removed for spectrographic analysis. The oils being used in the forgeries had been ordered through the account held by Danieli Restauro and then swapped out for an inferior brand in fake replica tubes; the original oils were then altered for use in the forgeries so that any chemical or spectrographic analysis would give results which were an exact match to the genuine article.

Giulia nodded approvingly at the artist then moved through to the back office, where strong chemical smells defeated the attempts of the air conditioning. Wrinkling her nose, she peered into a tray where sheets of paper sat in a solution designed to age the paper to a period appropriate state. A collection of dyes and inks sat nearby, while an elderly gentleman sat peering through a magnifying glass as he carefully carved the surface of a woodblock with a scalpel.

He nodded to Giulia. "We'll be ready for shipping at the end of the week. The first five paintings have been placed in age appropriate frames and crated for transit and the forgeries, hung in the original frames, have been returned to the Vasari corridor. These are lesser known works so the provenance is less detailed and easier to forge. It'll pass all but the most intense scrutiny. I just need to give the paper attached to the back of the panel a couple of days to oxidise then we're good to go."

"*Bene.* You have done well, all of you. I'll contact my husband and tell him to expect a shipment in a few days time. As soon as the works are received by the buyer and the funds transferred you'll be paid in full as discussed."

She returned to the studio, where the forger had taken a break. She sat herself in front of the facsimile oil and lifted the paints and brush. She smelled the linseed oil used to bind the pigments and considered the colour palette displayed before her. Azurite and ultramarine for blue. Vermilion and carmine lake for red. Naples and lead-tin yellow. A range of browns all obtained from umber. Lead white and lime white. Carbon black and bone black, the darkest colour of all. These were the essential pigments of the very greatest of artists, over generations and through changing styles, the major developments often merely reflecting subtle changes in balance, from the bright hues of the early Renaissance to the blacks and browns of Rembrandt's subdued tones.

She dipped her brush in the lead white and highlighted the leading edge of a glass, immediately producing a reflection, giving heightened sense of three dimensionality to the work. A dab of brown, thicker in consistency, added texture to the bread. A tiny spot of yellow and one would swear the peach had ripened just a touch. And yet, despite years of tuition, Giulia had come to realise she would never be an artist – not in the creative sense, at least. The ability to restore treasured works to their former splendour was, of course, a considerable consolation.

Her role in forgery and deception had become increasingly tainted. She had been led into the murky and odious reaches of art fraud while still in thrall to Tommaso, when he seemed charismatic and excitingly dangerous. Money came easily, at seemingly little risk and – well, no one was being hurt, surely? But now, her naivety galled her; it was never going to be something she could walk away from when she chose to, that should have been obvious from the outset. Tommaso was not the kind of man one could choose whether to obey and he had become over dependent on her, from access to materials, to using the institute as a vehicle for his projects, to the availability of her husband as broker and dealer in the Far East.

She made one, final, telling mark on the panel. A spot of bone black, apply subtle pressure in the centre of the peach. How easily the rot sets in.

Chapter 26
Florence
May 2018

Gianluca was the one driving things forward now. Both Marco and
Jeffrey had worked hard collecting evidence, pulling together
information which was beginning to build a compelling case against
Tommaso Rialo, but he was a dangerous opponent and they realised
lives had already been lost as he fought to cover his tracks. The open
secret that Detective Esposito was turning a blind eye to Tommaso's
nefarious activity now had some concrete evidence to back it up, but
reeling Esposito in would require subtle handling. Tommaso would be
perfectly happy to hang him out to dry and there was little to be gained
by exposing a washed-up cop on the point of retirement. Marco had
come up with an altogether more useful strategy.

He knew that Esposito would simply stonewall any attempts by himself
or Jeffrey to implicate him in enquiries against Tommaso. However,
Esposito could hardly decline an invitation from the security services to
be interviewed as part of a developing line of enquiry regarding the
magnate. Gianluca therefore submitted an official request that Esposito
make himself available for interview at the AISI offices in Florence. At
the allotted time, Marco and Jeffrey joined him in the interview room.

When Gianluca showed Esposito into the room, he was clearly taken
aback at the presence of the two men, who sat in the corners of the
room behind Gianluca. Esposito nodded to each as he walked around
the desk and took his seat, facing the three men. He composed his
features into a noncommittal stone face and reclined in his seat, lacing
his fingers over his corpulent stomach, a gesture which Jeffrey recalled
from his previous meeting with the detective and one which he
suspected divulged a high level of anxiety.

Gianluca shuffled some papers on the desk; they were blank but
Esposito didn't know that.
"I believe you know Jeffrey Sims, whose daughter was in your custody
a few days ago. This other gentleman," he gestured over his left

shoulder, "is Marco di Luca, an ex-intelligence officer who has been making enquiries into the affairs of Tommaso Rialo. Together we are collecting evidence which appears to implicate *Signore* Rialo in a range of criminal activities. We wanted to find out what information the police may have that could contribute to our investigation."

Esposito sat, silent and unmoving. He clearly was not going to offer any details up freely or voluntarily. Gianluca raised an eyebrow. "Detective?"

Esposito studied his hands. "There is much spoken about Tommaso Rialo. Much rumour and speculation. But, as you all know, suspicion and proof are two very different things. Tommaso is undoubtedly an extremely clever man. He also has some very powerful friends. We are not, nor ever have been, in possession of any evidence that would lead to Tommaso Rialo being charged with any crime. Do I *think* that he is involved in criminal activities? *Probablimente.* Can I *prove* anything?" He spread his hands in a gesture of defeat.

"Perhaps I can be more specific?" offered Gianluca, in his most obsequious tone. "We have evidence pointing to Tommaso's involvement in fraud, art forgery, money laundering and a recent sexual assault. Can the police enlighten us on any of these fronts?"

Esposito laughed out loud. "Well, gentlemen, you *have* been busy! And all still in remarkably good health by all appearances. Unfortunately, we mere mortals have been busy with two recent sudden and suspicious deaths. Perhaps, as you English say," here he looked pointedly at Jeffrey, "these are the eggs that get broken when one makes an omelette?"

Gianluca stared him out, until Esposito was forced to break his gaze. "I trust that those enquires will prove to be within your capabilities. The police have a reputation for concentrating on the more, how shall I say, *uncomplicated* aspects of local law enforcement but even you cannot ignore a homicide, no matter who may be behind it."

Esposito leaned forward, rattled and angry. "How dare you insinuate that? If you have anything to accuse me of, then come right out and say it!"

Gianluca paused for effect. "Of course. I believe that you deliberately and repeatedly turn a blind eye to matters involving Tommaso Rialo. At the very least, you refuse to look in his direction and, now, we have evidence that you have deliberately removed potentially incriminating evidence from the chain of an enquiry. Is that sufficiently clear and concise for you?"

Esposito rose to his feet, finger pointing across the desk. "You bastard! I'll sue for that, I'll have your badge!"

Gianluca waited a split second. "No, you won't. If you have any sense, you'll calm down, sit down and listen whilst we tell you how you're going to get out of this in one piece."

Esposito had turned an alarming shade of puce. He grasped the edge of the desk for support, sat down heavily in his seat and wiped his brow with a grubby handkerchief.

It was Marco who spoke next. "It's not you we're after, Luigi. We get it, your position, we do. You're months from retiring with distinction. You know that Tommaso Rialo has most of the city, including the police department, by the balls. It's been that way for years; if you try to change it now, you'll most likely never be alive to collect your pension. I'd probably do the same. We just need your help with one final piece of the puzzle. We're ready to move against Tommaso using the AISI and the Guardia di Finanza, but there's one final move against him that would come under your jurisdiction."

Esposito had recovered some of his colour and most of his bluster. "And why should I agree to help you? As you've just pointed out, I'd be signing my own death warrant. You can't prove I've done anything wrong. I'll just freewheel the last few months and wave you all goodbye. You can take your own chances with Tommaso."

Jeffrey spoke from the corner. "Do you remember our last meeting? When you told me you had no idea where and how my daughter's evidence had gone missing? That's not strictly true is it?" He rose and approached the desk, laying in front of Esposito the signed evidence receipt and his voice recorder; he pressed play as all four men listened to Dr. Riccardi's sullen tones fill the small room.

When the recording finished, Esposito was a broken man, sitting with his head in his hands.
"That's sufficient to have you brought up on charges and dismissed in disgrace, with no pension," said Gianluca, surprisingly gently. "Of course, we can offer you another way…"

Chapter 27
Florence
May 2018

The secretary at the Palazzo Moretti pressed the intercom. Tommaso Rialo answered in his customary short manner, *'Pronto'*.

'Il tuo ospite è arrivato'. He grinned, a lascivious leering look which made no secret of what thoughts were going through his mind. He looked in the mirror, straightened his tie and slicked back his oily hair. Fixing his most welcoming smile on his face, he sauntered out into the reception area, the epitome of *sprezzatura*.

His guest sat erect on one of the antique waiting room chairs, partly in anticipation of meeting the famous restorer but mainly because of how uncomfortable the chair was, especially after several hours in an airline seat. On seeing Tommaso, she rose and extended a well manicured hand in greeting. She was well aware of his reputation, so it was no surprise to her when he bowed his head and kissed the back of her hand, but the knowledge did not render the experience any less unpleasant.

"Welcome to Florence, *Signora* Chatwell. I trust you had a pleasant flight?"

"Thank you, *Signore* Rialo. We were somewhat delayed – I hope I haven't detained you this evening?"

Tommaso brushed off the suggestion with an imperious wave. "Of course not. It's an honour to welcome such an esteemed colleague to view the work underway in the Palazzo Vecchio. I'm assuming you have seen Bronzino's work in the *capella* before?"

She smiled and nodded. "Indeed, but it was many years ago. It's a tremendous opportunity to see the restoration work in progress and to be able to examine such exquisite beauty at close quarters. Will we be able to visit the site this evening?"

"Of course, our team are expecting us and have cleared some of the equipment from the chapel to afford us a better view. Afterwards, I shall have my driver take you to your hotel so that you can refresh yourself. Then may I take you to dinner?"

She groaned inwardly, not relishing an evening of being fawned over, but smiled her agreement, as if nothing could possibly come close in terms of fulfilling her dreams.

~

Inside the apartments of Eleanora, all was quiet. The restorers had gone home early, leaving only the foreman on site, responsible for admitting Tommaso and Mrs. Chatwell, then locking up the premises for the evening. They sauntered through the four rooms dedicated to the lives of famous women, Tommaso taking considerable time to point out the thematic details on the ceilings and friezes of each, a process which appeared to necessitate repeated touches on Mrs. Chatwell's back and shoulders. Soon, they arrived in the *camera verde*, which was crammed full of equipment which had been placed carefully against the walls, affording excellent views of the Chapel of Eleanora. Mrs. Chatwell drank in the beauty of the place, mentally mapping the frescoes onto the visual framework she had worked so hard to imprint in her mind. The process was considerably simplified by the fact that Tommaso treated the visit more akin to showing off a new car to a fawning admirer than having an academic discussion with a professional equal. Recognising the sight and sound of an unstoppable ego in full flow, she was happy to sit back and listen.

It was, indeed, a magnificent sight. Inspecting those portions of the frescoes that remained in their original condition, one would never have imagined that they were discoloured and partly damaged. It was only when one drank in the kaleidoscopic colours and jewel-like clarity of the restored surfaces that the transformation became apparent. They had restored approximately one third of the left hand wall frescoes of Moses striking the rock. Mrs. Chatwell sought and located the familiar figure of the pregnant woman standing behind Moses. "Is it true that that is a depiction of Eleanora?"

Tommaso nodded sagely. "Indeed yes. When the chapel was being built and frescoed, between 1540 and 1545, Eleanora was performing her motherly duties and bringing a child into the world every year. One assumes she asked Bronzino to commemorate her fecundity in perpetuity."

Mrs. Chatwell hesitated before speaking, but decided it was the right thing to do. "I read about your son. I'm so sorry, that must have been very difficult for you."

He visibly stiffened; when he spoke it was in a low growl. "It was, and still is, a time of much sadness and regret." Clearly regarding the matter, and indeed the visit, at an end, he gestured imperiously to the foreman to close up and led Mrs. Chatwell out of the chapel.

~

He took a long pull on his brandy and lit up one of his Tuscan cigars, blowing out a satisfied cloud of blue smoke. It had been an enjoyable meal in one of his favourite restaurants, designed to impress his guest. The owner had fawned around him, as he always did, and Tommaso had pushed the boat out a little on some very expensive wine. He had tipped the waiter to keep filling his companion's glass and, indeed, she now seemed much more relaxed and a little giggly. He had, out of politeness, made reference to her work, having gained a very superficial knowledge thereof by skimming through her Facebook and LinkedIn pages, but it appeared that she wasn't really that interested in talking about herself, preferring instead to bring things back to learning of his work in the institute. Of course, that presented no issues; talking about himself was something that Tommaso both enjoyed and excelled in.

The outside *terrazzo* at *Rivoire* was the perfect location for the final part of the evening (well, he hoped, perhaps the penultimate). Timeless and elegant, its exorbitant prices meant that, particularly late of an evening, its clientele reflected the upper end of the local population rather than the tourist masses which plagued the city by day. The *Piazza della Signoria* was, indeed, quiet now, mostly populated by couples gently strolling arm in arm, perhaps exploring the sculptures in the *Loggia dei Lanzi*. The Palazzo Vecchio seemed even more foreboding and impressive after dark, he always thought, as if it thrust out the darker side of its nature; bodies of traitors hanging from its walls, screams of prisoners offering up confessions under torture. Yes, his beloved Florence had its sinister side, as he very well knew.

Across the table, Mrs. Chatwell stifled a yawn. "Oh, excuse *me,* it's been a long day!"

He smiled, showing his small, sharp teeth. "Of course. I have detained you too long. May I escort you back to your hotel?"

She smiled warmly and he rose, a sweep of his arm inviting her to precede him. They strolled in silence along Via dei Calzaiuoli and within moments stopped outside a hotel. "This is me," said Mrs. Chatwell, stopping and making no attempt to go inside. She paused, offering up a moment. This was going to be easy, almost *too* easy. He paused, like a lion before an antelope, savouring the moment before he pounced. "Would you care to come up for a nightcap?" she asked. He flashed those teeth again as if tasting his triumph.

~

It was a deceptively large suite, for what seemed from the street to be a small hotel. She invited him to pour them a drink from the minibar as she slipped next door to the bedroom. He imagined he heard a lock turn and wondered why she needed to lock the bathroom door when she was so clearly submitting to his attentions. Anyway, another brandy for him, gin and tonic for her. A large one. These were the moments he relished most, just before the conquest. He heard her returning; she hadn't changed, he saw with a flash of annoyance, still all buttoned up tight. Even so, all the more fun to be had.

She came and sat on the sofa with her back to the bedroom, opposite where he was sitting. Playing hard to get, he thought. What fun. He rose, carrying a drink in each hand and moved to sit down beside her. She didn't make it easy by shuffling to one end of the sofa; instead she perched awkwardly in the middle. Come on, he thought, enough pretending – time to let go and enjoy yourself. He wedged himself in beside her and threw an arm over the back of the sofa, around her shoulder, and pulled her towards him.

Or at least attempted to, but she was fighting against him, daring to push him away. "I think perhaps you've misunderstood me," she whined, pathetically. "Maybe you should go now?"

He pushed back. "What do you mean? You know this is what you want. You asked me here for a reason, you know what that is. Stop messing around." He pulled her towards him and clumsily tried to kiss her. She slapped him and tried to stand up.

"I said stop and I meant it! You need to stop what you're doing and leave now!"

His temper was up now. He pulled at her dress, trying to pull down the zip at the back. There was a tearing sound as the fabric ripped. Her necklace was torn from her neck; he callously threw it across the room. She succeeded in rising from the sofa, but he caught her hand and pulled her back towards him.

"Stop, you bastard!" she screamed, slapping ineffectually at him.

He laughed, enjoying the thrill of the chase. She slapped him hard across the face, her ring catching a flap of skin and drawing blood. Time stood still; both froze, consumed by the enormity of the moment.

"You bitch," he growled, a mixture of anger and arousal. "I'll fuck you hard for that, till you beg me to stop!"

"She's already asked you to stop. Several times in fact," said a voice from behind Tommaso. "And you didn't. Which makes it sexual assault. Or attempted rape, depending on which prosecutor we get. Stand back at once, sir."

Tommaso whirled round to see Detective Esposito aiming his gun at him. Beside him, recording everything on a video camera, was Jeffrey Sims. "Are you ok, darling?" he asked solicitously.

Mrs. 'Chatwell' glared poison at Tommaso. "I'm fine thank you, darling. But that's four hours of my life I'll never get back. I feel I need a shower to wash any trace of this bastard away. Hopefully this'll mean that no other poor woman has to submit to this monster ever again."

Esposito smiled. "That's exactly our intention Mrs. Sims."

Chapter 28
Florence
May 2018

Marco had longed for this moment for years. When he had stood by Marianna's graveside as they lowered her coffin into the ground, he had vowed to topple Tommaso Rialo and his evil regime. For years, he had been forced to watch and wait as, in plain view, the magnate had strutted like a peacock, revelling in both the attention he attracted and the misery he caused. Life after life had been ground underfoot as he ruthlessly built his drug empire and laundered its proceeds right under the noses of the authorities.

He was clever, no doubt. A cordon of enforcers had intimidated not only the population of the city but the police force itself into turning a blind eye to even the most flagrant of abuses. Tommaso had enlisted the very best computer fraud experts to create a filigree of financial pathways capable of moving funds around the world in a money laundering network so sophisticated as to be virtually undetectable. His ability to produce replica works of art to the highest of standards provided the perfect vehicle for transferring large sums of money. Ironically, it was precisely because he was so well known and celebrated a figure that he could pull off such an audacious high wire act. But now, he was about to take a fall and there was no safety net waiting.

~

Fittingly, it was Lucrezia, one of Tommaso's most recent and most despicable victims, who set the wheels in motion. Sitting with Giulia, shedding crocodile tears, she let slip the story that Marco was moving in to arrange for Tommaso's assets to be seized. Blissfully unaware of her role in her partner's downfall, Giulia duly alerted Tommaso. He was caught in the horns of a dilemma; were they trying to smoke him out? Uncharacteristically for him, he acted rashly and began the process of transferring funds to a shell company in Taiwan, which the Guardia Di Finanza had identified as they had built up the portfolio of

Tommaso's companies. As soon as the funds were transferred the Guardia sequestered them and locked the data trail tight.

~

At the other side of the world, Antonio Bianchi was at Freeport Singapore to take delivery of a crate freighted from Rome. The tracker attached to the crate by AISI revealed that it had been transported by rail from Florence to Fiumicino airport before being flown to the Far East via Dubai. The paper trail was in order; delivery of six modern art works purchased by a billionaire Chinese collector to be stored in the Freeport facility. Officials of the Commercial Affairs Department of the Singapore police were on hand with a search warrant entitling them to open the crate on suspicion that the contents were original Renaissance portraits. Their suspicions were correct; Antonio Bianchi was arrested and charged with handling stolen goods.

~

Danieli Restauro was raided by Florentine detectives, who seized invoices relating to purchases of art materials and samples of the actual paints and pigments. Spectrographic analysis confirmed that the paints were of an inferior quality and an exact match to samples taken from works which had been renovated in the establishment's workshops and then proven to have deteriorated. The chief procurer of supplies was arrested on suspicion of fraud and agreed to testify against Tommaso Rialo, in return for a reduced sentence. He asked for similar offences in two other Florentine restoration premises, subsequently closed down by crippling litigation cases, to be taken into consideration.

~

Esposito himself led the raid on the studio where the forgeries were created. He was ashamed of himself for kowtowing to Tommaso for so long; he had been a coward as people had suffered and died. Once this was all over, he was going to hand in his badge and retire. Too late for many, he acknowledged, but one last chance to do the right thing was presented to him now.

The squad had been tipped off that the first of a new batch of works had been removed from the Vasari corridor that night and brought to the workshop. All was quiet when the team arrived; only a ribbon of light from below the door gave any indication of the room being occupied. At a nod from Esposito, two officers swung the battering ram and the door flew open. The astonished forgers were overpowered in seconds and led away in handcuffs as the crime scene team swept in to gather evidence.

~

Lucrezia sat listening as the exchanges between Giulia and Tommaso became increasingly belligerent. The normally suave businessman was rapidly losing the *sprezzatura* he normally prided himself on. His erstwhile partner in crime rapidly became the subject of his ire as he rounded on her, providing a litany of failings and broken promises. Moment by moment he tightened the noose around both their necks, blissfully unaware that every word was being recorded and listened to by Gianluca in AISI headquarters, who grinned from ear to ear.

~

Marco had wanted to see their faces as the final trap was set. He inserted the USB stick on which his colleague had downloaded the software written to reset the CCTV which Tommaso had overwritten. He called up the images of the *camera verde* and *Capella di Eleanora,* empty and silent. With a flourish, he pressed 'enter' on the computer and, immediately, the image changed to show two men removing a painting from its frame and passing it to a third, who placed it on the flatbed of a large scanner. Marco smiled and waved at the screen, enjoying the moment, even though they couldn't see him. Licking his lips in anticipation, he keyed the location of the rooms involved into the security system and, with a flourish, hit the alarm pad, satisfyingly depicted on screen as a giant red button.

A cacophony of sirens erupted, causing the men on screen to jump and drop what they were doing. As if pursued by demons, they ran through the door into the Vasari corridor. Marco imagined the scene as they fled, over the bridge that crossed the road far below, then sharp right along the *lungarno* before turning left above the Ponte Vecchio. They wouldn't stop to look out over the Arno to Ponte Santa Trinita or into beautiful Santa Felicita; no, they would hare on, over the roofs of the houses on the *oltrarno,* finally reaching the Boboli Gardens and the gate that led them out adjacent to the Buontalenti Grotto. They'd be bursting out of that gate, to which they always had a key, right about now, Marco reckoned. Right into the faces of a fully armed squadron of his ex colleagues from AISI, all of whom he'd personally invited to enjoy the moment.

~

Giulia's phone rang. It was over, she knew it was. There was actually a huge sense of relief that the pretence was coming to an end. It had long since stopped been fun, being glamorous – like they showed it in the movies. It had become a smutty, unsavoury existence, dancing to the tune of a man with whom she had once, what seemed like a lifetime ago, been in love. Hidden under layers of tarnish was a faint recollection of enchantment and excitement, but that was before the brutal recognition that people were paying a heavy price for her hedonism. Most recently of all, Lucrezia, a young woman, full of life, who shared her love of art and exemplified her own ideals of feminine strength and guile; she had allowed her to be ruthlessly violated and then had stood aside as her father took the fall. In many ways, it was a blessing that it would soon all be over…

It was Tommaso who was calling. Why? Surely he knew all the traps had been sprung at once; even for him, the greatest dissembler she had ever known, the game was up. He had a quote from Machiavelli above his desk: "Everyone sees what you appear to be, few experience what you really are." Her feelings towards Tommaso were better captured by another quote from the great man: "It is better to be feared than loved, if you cannot be both."

She answered, hearing his gruff, defiant voice one last time. *"Ti amo."* Then she heard a single gunshot.

Chapter 29
Florence
June 2018

They stood together in the confined space, marvelling at its beauty. Somehow, this tranquil place of meditation seemed a fitting location to reflect on all that they had been through in such a short period of time. From the depths of conflict and despair had come the most unlikely of resurrections, the healing of divisions, the restoration of hope. None of the three believed in a higher power and all quietly contemplated the inner strength that each had found to fulfil their roles in the rebirth of their family.

"It's hard to believe this is a facsimile," said Lucrezia as she emerged from the reproduction of the *Capella di Eleanora.* From the outside, the aluminium framework and fibreglass panels looked like something from a building site, but as soon as one stepped inside the candlelit interior the quality of the reproduction was truly breathtaking. The company in charge of the 3D scanners had stepped in to take control of the project after Tommaso's death, pressing home the fact that any publicity is good publicity and cognisant of the fact that the whole of Eleanora's apartments were now a crime scene and that the completion of the renovation project would be significantly delayed. At least the visitors to the city could appreciate the beauty of the *Capella* in its new permanent location, adjacent to Bronzino's 'Last Supper' in the refectory of San Salviati.

Marie smiled. "It's certainly more enjoyable than my visit to the real thing with that despicable man Rialo. I have *no* idea how I managed to pull that off!"

Jeffrey put his arm around his wife's waist and pulled her close. "You were magnificent, darling," he whispered affectionately. "I'm so sorry you had to do that."

"Well, *I'm* not," she said, defiantly. "We all had our parts to play in bringing that man to justice, after what he put you both through."

Jeffrey was not yet entirely comfortable with the shift in his wife's perception, that he was no longer sinner but, instead, sinned against. He had perhaps reached midpoint in that paradigm shift but it was very much a work in progress.

Lucrezia, on the other hand, had clearly reached a later stage in her metamorphosis. She stood, hand in hand, with Stefano, admiring the 'Last Supper', deep in animated conversation. They had spent long hours sharing their fears that the dual trauma of her assault at the hands of Tommaso (although thankfully she still had no recollection of the night's events) and the calculated deception worked by Giulia might traumatise her, drive her deep inside herself and thwart her ambition. In fact, the opposite had occurred; she appeared galvanised into action with a new found enthusiasm for life.

The staff at Advancing Women Artists, themselves in shock at the extent of Giulia's misdemeanours, took Lucrezia to their hearts and offered to tutor her in the restoration techniques she was so desperate to learn. Most of the academic curriculum, and all of the restoration work, at the Palazzo Moretti was on hold as the criminal investigation into Tommaso's business dealing meant that the assets there had been frozen. AWA had been so impressed by Lucrezia's ability and application that they had taken her on as an employee while funding her Masters in Art Conservation and Restoration. She had a guaranteed three years paid employment with the likelihood of a degree which would help her get a job in cultural heritage anywhere in the world.

Florence had taken hold of her heart, despite the inauspicious beginning to her stay. A large part of that, recently, had been Stefano, one of the quieter students on the course, but the one who had made it clear, quietly and persistently, that he was there to support Lucrezia, in any way she asked, no strings attached. He had listened attentively at all hours of day or night, often saying nothing, because that was what was required, but having an unerring ability to contribute a helpful, compassionate insight, just when it was most needed. Their communication had been almost telepathic at times. The terrible betrayal by Tommaso, which reawakened memories of her callous rejection years before, had completely undermined her faith in men; Stefano recognised that and stoically set about building the foundations of trust, on which Lucrezia herself erected a bedrock of friendship and then build the capacity to invite intimacy into her life once more.

Both Jeffrey and Marie had instantly liked the boy to whom their daughter had, somewhat to their surprise, opened her heart. He was unerringly supportive, charming to the point of being gallant, and ineffably wise. Jeffrey, in particular, found he was almost of a bygone age, the sort of young man who would pledge to deliver your daughter home by ten and then turn up at five minutes to. He was immeasurably relieved by that. As if sensing the approval, Stefano and Lucrezia walked over, hand in hand.

As the group assembled, they noticed Marco arriving, hands in pockets, in his usual unassuming way. He knew that Jeffrey and Marie were flying home the next day and had wanted to mark the farewell. He hadn't said much during the process of Tommaso's death and Giulia's arrest, and the considerable publicity that surrounded the case, with the headline grabbing links to art forgery and money laundering. Jeffrey had, several times, attempted to get him to accept a fee for his services, but he had repeatedly declined to do so. He said that seeing the demise of Tommaso was reward enough; everyone knew he had personal reasons for doing so but he never came close to sharing them.

Stefano bounced over and shook his hand; they had become particularly close in recent days.
"So, Marco, have you thought it over? Will you coach us? With your help, the *azzuri* can win this year!" Marco laughed and ruffled his hair. "I knew you were serious, *amico,* when you stopped smoking! Or is that for the benefit of a certain young lady?"

Stefano grinned from ear to ear. "Two benefits from one small concession. I get to snuggle up without being told I stink and I'm fit to captain the winning team in *calcio!*"

Jeffrey was looking completely bemused. Stefano came to his rescue. "*Calcio Fiorentino* - it's a sixteenth century game a bit like a mixture between football, rugby and open warfare, played in Piazza Santa Croce every year. The *azzuri,* the blues, are from the Santa Croce quarter, my area. Marco used to play handball for Italy and he's going to coach us and maybe even play!"

Marco had both hands up in mock surrender. "Whoa there, I'm not *that* crazy! People get hurt in that madness, I'm far too old to get out of the way in time. If you want this old dog to teach you pups some moves, that's fine by me. But don't come crying to me if you get hurt!"

Stefano offered up a high five, which Marco accepted with a grin, then walked back with Lucrezia towards the fresco. Jeffrey came and offered his hand, which Marco took, with both his, in a firm grip. "Thank you, with all my heart, for what you have done for my daughter." He was close to tears.

Marco nodded, silently. Then, after a moment, he looked at Jeffrey. "You have changed, my friend. You arrived a beaten man and, when they kicked you when you were down, you just rolled over expecting more. But then something happened, a fire built within you and you stood up and came through for your family. I hope you feel very proud."

It was the longest speech any of them had heard Marco make. Jeffrey stood, nonplussed for a moment, then replied quietly. "Perhaps that will come. At the moment I'm just a little less ashamed, and that's something to begin with. My family is reunited and that's all I could ever have asked for."

With a nod, Marco turned and was gone.

Marie looked at the man with whom she had shared her life, a man who had seemed lost to her forever, but who had now found his way back into her heart. She felt an immense sense of relief and a small glow of pride at the role she had played in serving justice. But her greatest joy was the new found determination in her daughter to be recognised as an individual with strengths and talents. As a mother, she had always known that those qualities were there, but suspected that Lucrezia had, to an extent, coasted along, fulfilling the role expected of a daughter of two lauded academics. *Of course* she would go to university, get a degree, everyone had said. She's Jeffrey and Marie's *daughter*. But now, she had elected to step out into the world on her own terms, asking to be noticed and respected in her own rights. It was a thrilling sight. As a historian, Marie could think of several famous women who had made the same transition, but none seemed more apt than Eleanora of Toledo, who, four hundred and sixty odd years ago, in this very city, had stepped out of the shadow of Cosimo, Grand Duke of Tuscany, and made her own indelible mark on history.

Printed in Great Britain
by Amazon

59320421R00095